Vanishing Tra

Patrick Lindsay

Copyright 2020

Cover Design: SelfPubBookCovers.com / VonnaArt

Table of Contents

Chapter

19. Home at the Ranch

Prologue

Holt Jacobs hunched down among the oak trees and studied the corral in front of him through his binoculars. He considered himself a fine judge of horses, and he had pretty much decided on the palomino mare and the tall gray gelding. He studied the gelding a moment longer. He guessed it must be a little over sixteen hands.

He swept his glasses over the other five horses in the corral, then returned to the original two. He grunted in satisfaction, put the binoculars away, and rolled over on his back to wait for darkness to settle in. If it were up to him, he would steal at least four of those horses, and maybe all of them. It wasn't up to him, he reminded himself.

His orders came from someone he just referred to as The Boss. Holt had the impression The Boss was pretty respectable, maybe a pretty big man in one of these towns around here. He never got his hands dirty with the horse stealing. He had Holt to take care of that for him. Holt had actually never met or seen The Boss. He only got messages addressed to him at a hotel in Austin where he checked in once in a while. When the horses were delivered, his share was given to him in cash at the drop-off place, and the rest was sent to The Boss in some way. That end of the operation was run through another man, but Holt intended to find out more about it.

A noise in the corral caught his attention, and he rolled over to check things out. A cowboy was returning from his day's work. He unsaddled his horse, rubbed it down, and turned it loose in the corral before heading for the bunkhouse. The door slammed shut behind the cowboy and things got quiet again.

Satisfied that his two theft targets were still in the corral, Holt Jacobs turned over onto his back again and waited quietly for full darkness to arrive and for everybody to settle down and go to bed in the house and bunkhouse. He had to admit, he reflected, that life was better since he'd been working for The Boss, whoever he was.

There were posters out on him throughout Arizona and parts of New Mexico. He'd not seen or heard of any posters in Texas, and that was fine with him. Especially, he thought, because the reward for him was of the "Dead or Alive" variety. He had, by his own count, killed seventeen men in fair, stand-up gun fights. He didn't mind the gunfights, in fact he kind of liked them. Nobody had ever bested him, and he didn't mind the killing. It was the being hunted part that had worn him down.

The horse thieving had kept him pretty much out of sight, and the pay was pretty good. His time was his own in between jobs, and he had several places he liked to frequent in Austin and San Antonio. It bothered him a little that he had to travel so far to each place where he was sent to steal the horses, and all of those places were pretty far away from the hideout. Still, he had to admit that The Boss had it organized pretty well, and life was pretty good. He didn't really want to do anything else for a while.

When the darkness had settled in, and the lanterns in the house and bunkhouse had been put out quite some time ago, he eased from his hiding spot and tiptoed toward the corral. He paused when the horses caught his scent and snorted, but they settled down pretty quickly and he worked his way over to the gate. The moonlight proved enough visibility to ease the gate open and slip in inside.

He shook out a loop on the rope he'd brought with him. The palomino mare proved docile enough that he was able to walk up quietly and slip the noose over her head. He led her over and tied her to the rail near the gate. Taking down another rope that he'd observed earlier, hanging over a fence post, he moved toward the tall gelding. This one proved to be a little more suspicious of him, snorting and tossing his head, then moving away.

Having neither the time nor the patience to slip up on the gelding, he shook out a loop and tossed it over the horse's head, speaking soothingly and casting a few anxious glances over his shoulder, first at the bunkhouse, then at the ranch house. His luck seemed to be holding; he saw no lights inside. He led the gelding quietly over to the gate where he slipped the knot loose on the rope holding the mare and led them both out of the corral. He briefly considered scattering the other horses, but decided the noise might cause too much trouble. He eased the gate shut and latched it behind him.

Leading the horses steadily out of the yard, he worked his way into the trees, headed for the place where he had tethered his own horse several hours earlier. The light cast by the full moon helped him again, and he found his horse quickly. He tied both stolen horses to his saddle horn and led them away. He planned to ride for several hours, stopping to cover his trail now and then, before he stopped for a little sleep. He wanted to be well away from any possible pursuit.

Feeling something strike him on the cheek, Holt's eyes fluttered open, and he rolled instinctively off the bedroll, reaching under it for his gun. Bright sunlight caused him to squint, and he stayed in the crouched position, blinking furiously and trying to orient himself. He eventually registered a chattering noise overhead and looked upward to see a squirrel scolding him and dashing back and forth on a tree limb. He looked down to see several acorns lying beside his bedroll.

He stood, rubbing his eyes, and put the gun away. He moved to a small campfire he had made, about ten feet away, and made preparations for coffee and some bacon. He chewed a biscuit absently as he rolled up the bedroll and tied it to the saddle. He glanced overhead, frowning. He had clearly slept quite a bit later than he'd planned.

He finished a quick breakfast and moved out to the west, anticipating a meeting at the hideout sometime tonight. He'd hired a couple ne'er-do-wells to keep an eye on the place and look after the horses until he could move them for sale. He paid them as little as possible. If they got greedy or too curious, he had ways of moving them on. Holt was a small man, but they feared his guns.

He glanced down before mounting his horse, a frown breaking out on his face as he looked at his boot print. His feet were exceptionally small, and it was a sore point with him. He had even killed a man once for making jokes about his "peg-leg" boot print. He swore under his breath and stepped up into the saddle. He had some ground to make up after his late start.

Leading the two stolen horses as he had done the previous night, Jacobs struck off again to the west, stopping to splash across a stream whenever he found one, feeling confident he could soon shake off any pursuit. He had to admit this is where it came in handy to steal only two horses. The owners were less likely to keep up the pursuit when the loss was comparatively small. Unless, he conceded, he had stolen someone's prize mount. Then they might pursue for a long time.

Moving up into some low hills, he took a break for a few minutes and watched his back trail. He tethered the horses and lay down at the top of a ridge, breaking out the binoculars and looking down over the ground he had just covered. He swept the glasses back and forth, then stopped to stare at a small dust trail in the distance. He focused on the spot where the dust had risen. He again swore softly to himself. A single man was riding along slowly, leaning over to read the tracks in the dust. Holt caught the glint of a badge in the sun.

Laying the binoculars aside, he ran over the possibilities in his head. He didn't want to run for it. The man was a pretty good tracker to have followed him this far. He prided himself on what he could do in a standup gunfight, but there was no point in letting it come to that. He needed to kill this man and move out. He stood and walked to his horse, pulling the Winchester from the scabbard and returning to lie down at the top of the ridge. Now he would wait.

He waited for an hour, watching the pursuer cast back and forth along a creek until he picked up the trail on the other side. He came on, looking up into the small hills in front of him from time to time. Holt made sure not to let anything metallic reflect a glare from the overhead sun. As the man drew closer, he pulled his Winchester in front of him and sighted carefully down the barrel. He exhaled slowly and gently squeezed the trigger.

The lawman, or whoever he was, pitched backward off the saddle and his horse bolted several yards. Holt Jacobs grabbed the binoculars and looked at the spot where the man had fallen. The man attempted to rise, not even reaching his knees before he fell and rolled over onto his back. He lay still.

Holt remained motionless for several minutes, sweeping the area with the binoculars. He felt sure the man below was dead, but he wanted to be sure there was no one else who had heard the shot and investigated. Finally, convinced that no one else was coming, he rose, mounted, and rode down to look at the man he had shot.

When he reached the spot and dismounted, he approached the body cautiously, pistol in his hand, looking around him. He prodded the body with his foot and got no response. Holstering his gun, he knelt down and looked at the man. He was sure he had never seen this man before. He reached down and pulled the Texas Rangers badge from his shirt, then pocketed it. The longer he could keep anybody from knowing he had killed a Ranger, the better. He found a little money in the man's shirt and pocketed that as well. He covered the man's face with his hat.

Finally, he stood and re-mounted his horse, staring down at the corpse. A shock of bright red hair peaked out from under the man's hat. That, he knew, might be a dead giveaway in helping them identify the dead man. He shrugged and turned the horse to ride away. There was nothing he could do about the red hair.

Chapter One
Ash McKinnon

Langtry, Texas
January 1883

I stood at the bar in an open tent saloon and surveyed the surrounding spectacle. A sign hung above the entrance of the tent with words proclaiming "Law West of the Pecos". A smaller sign to the side identified the place as "The Jersey Lilly". Several doubtful-looking characters were lined up at the bar beside me. The first was my partner in the Texas Rangers, Charlie Bass, and the rest were railroad workers or travelers passing through town. Most of us were drinking beer; a few had the misfortune of trying the house whiskey.

The activity caught my attention at the far end of the tent. This, I had learned, was a combination saloon and court room. Judge Roy Bean was holding court down there, and it appeared to be a wedding. I heard him asking the man and woman some pretty standard questions, and there were mumbled answers that I couldn't quite make out. Finally, the judge grabbed his gavel and raised it in the air. I leaned forward, knowing what he would say next.

Roy Bean slammed the gavel down and bellowed, "I pronounce you man and wife. May God have mercy on your souls!" With that, he shepherded the happy couple toward the bar and let them know they were expected to buy whiskey, besides the five dollars they owed him for the wedding.

I snorted into my beer and turned back around to the bar. Never having gotten married myself, I couldn't be certain, but I was pretty sure the "God have mercy on your souls" part wasn't something you would generally hear at a wedding. Seeing the judge headed in my direction, I slid my five cents across the counter and got myself a refill. The judge didn't like to see empty glasses, and this was the only place to get a beer for miles.

My name is Ash McKinnon, and I have been a Texas Ranger for about a year and a half now. They recruited me after a cattle drive from Central Texas to Kansas. It turned out that a Ranger named Red Corbin was one of the men on the drive. He had arranged for me to be hired by the Rangers, along with a friend named Mike Stone, because he liked the way we had handled ourselves on the drive.

I come from the hills in Tennessee, mighty close to North Carolina. Most folks have never heard of Ford Creek, the town I'm from, so I just say I'm from the hills in Tennessee. My ma claims I was big enough to sit at the dinner table when I was born. I don't know about that, but I stand about six feet three, and weigh in at 235 pounds. People and things generally get out of my way when I want them to. I might also mention that my granny says I'm good lookin', on account of my brown eyes and dark curly hair, but you know her eyesight ain't what it used to be.

I've spent three of my twenty-six years in Texas now, and I reckon I'll stay here. I had been sent out here to West Texas just a few months before, mainly to deal with bandidos from the south stealing cattle and horses from the ranchers in this remote area. Also, the railroad appreciated having a Ranger's presence if it was needed. It had been pretty quiet, all things considered. Quiet wasn't bad, but I felt a little cut off out here. My major source of entertainment had been watching Roy Bean conduct his "court".

A disturbance down the line at the bar got my attention. I saw a man standing at the bar, arguing with Roy Bean. I knew that wasn't generally a good idea. I hadn't seen the man around here before, and he was dressed too nice to be a railroad worker, cowboy, or drifting miner. I had a feeling they had overcharged him for his beer. Bean fleeced the strangers around town sometimes. I exchanged a glance with my partner, Charlie Bass. So far, we had stayed out of these things, not really knowing what our authority was around town.

The stranger raised his voice. "I gave you a twenty-dollar gold piece for a beer. Where's my change?"

Roy Bean polished a glass absently and stared at the newcomer. "You kin have a refill. Just holler."

The stranger was turning slightly red around the gills. "I don't want another beer! Look at that sign!" He pointed at a sign behind the bar, proclaiming beer for sale at 5 cents per glass. He waved his finger back and forth for emphasis.

Bean didn't bother to turn around and look at the sign. "This is my bar," he announced loudly. "Also, it's my court." He pointed at the Law West of the Pecos sign. "I like to keep the peace around here. It don't seem to me you're bein' peaceful." He slammed the glass down on the bar and leaned over the counter. "You need to pipe down."

The stranger, completely red in the face and almost at a loss for words, leaned in to get face-to-face with Roy Bean. "Where's my change?" he shouted. "You owe me $19.95."

Bean leaned down, fished around under the bar, and came up with a gavel. I glanced over at Charlie. We had no idea he kept a gavel under there. Bean lifted it up and rapped it down sharply on the counter. "I'm finin' you $19.95 for disturbin' the peace," he thundered. "I'd advise you to go back outside an' get on your train. If'n you disturb the peace any more, I'll be chaining you to that tree out there." He pointed toward a large ash tree outside the bar. "That there is my jail," he finished.

The stranger whirled around, looked at the ash tree, then looked around the tent, hoping for some help from somebody. No takers. Nobody looked in his direction. Finally, he drained his beer, slammed the glass down on the bar and headed off toward the train station.

"Probably a good idea," I observed. "No fun gettin' chained to that tree, I expect."

Charlie finished his beer, then glanced over in my direction. "Don't never let him chain me to that tree, McKinnon," he said.

"It's a deal," I agreed, finishing my glass and moving out of the tent with Charlie. "We don't pay more than a nickel for a beer around here, and we don't let each other get chained to that tree." Sometimes, I thought, it's good to wear a star on your shirt. Even Roy Bean hadn't tried to mess with us yet.

We left the Jersey Lilly/courthouse and ambled down to what passed for a main street in Langtry. We hitched our horses outside the only café in town. The menu ran heavily to beef and beans, but it beat anything Charlie and I might be cooking. Before stopping in to eat, we were interested in getting any mail that might have come in on today's train. There was no post office out here, nor was there a telegraph office. News came once a week in the mail on the train.

We lined up outside what passed for a railroad office. There was a tent stretched out next to the tracks. There was a table under an awning outside the tent, and once a week they passed out mail. The wind kicked up heavy swirls of dust in the street as we waited. December and January were the driest months of the year around here, and we had just come through an exceptionally dry six weeks. I had to admit there were times when I longed for those green hills of Tennessee.

At long last I heard my name called and stepped up to the table to take the letter they held out for me. A quick glance told me the letter was from the captain of our division, Samuel McMurry. Most of the rest of our division, Company B Frontier Battalion, was stationed in El Paso. I glanced quickly at Charlie as I tore the letter open and slowly began to read.

I was to report to Captain Bill McDonald in Austin for reassignment. Charlie Bass, my partner, was to rejoin the rest of our unit in El Paso. I looked up from the letter and caught his questioning glance. "You're to report back to the unit in El Paso," I told him. "I'm going to Austin."

I looked back down at the orders, and the next sentence jumped out at me. "Red Corbin has been killed," it said. "Catch the first train to Austin and report to Captain McDonald immediately." I reread the sentence, my lips moving wordlessly, then stared off down the street. Red had recruited me into the Texas Rangers and had pretty much taught me everything I knew about bein' a Ranger. A few memories of working with Red on the cattle drive, then on assignments with the Rangers swirled through my head.

I took a couple steps back toward the railroad office and read the handwritten sign posted at the tent entrance. The next train east left in two hours. I looked around to see Charlie watching me, saying nothing. I moved across the street. "I'm having another drink," I said to him over my shoulder. We both moved back into the Jersey Lilly. Looked like Judge Bean was done with court for the day.

The Southern Pacific line from Langtry back to San Antonio was close to empty on this trip. I sat alone in my row, huddled next to the window and staring out at some pretty dry, empty landscape as we rattled our way through West Texas. Being originally from Tennessee, I welcomed the idea of getting back to the hilly country around Austin, but I wondered why it was me they were bringing back to look into Red's death.

Following a cattle drive to Kansas, I had worked with Red, among others, on a case involving an old confederate of Sam Bass by the name of Louis Sharpe. Following a series of train robberies and bank robberies, we had tracked Sharpe to an area just north of Austin. On a piece of land belonging to my friend and fellow Ranger Mike Stone, we had caught up to Sharpe. Stone had killed him in a gunfight in the middle of a small creek on that property. I had been reassigned to the frontier division shortly after and hadn't seen Red since that time.

I was still wrestling with memories and questions as the shadows lengthened outside the train and darkness closed in. It would be late tomorrow before we arrived in San Antonio. I would probably need to stay there overnight and then catch another train to Austin. I reached up and pulled down my bedroll from the rack above me to serve as a pillow. I laid it between me and the window, then composed myself to get the best night's sleep I could under the circumstances.

Sleep hadn't come easily on the train to San Antonio. I kept remembering Red Corbin and some good times on the drive to Kansas. I wondered how he had been killed and whether they wanted me to track his killer. If so, why me? I wondered if my old friend Mike Stone would be assigned to the case. I had arrived at San Antonio completely exhausted. A night's stay at a hotel near the train station had helped. I was on my way to Austin now and figured I should arrive in a couple hours.

When the train pulled in, and I was no more settled in my mind than I had been two days before, when the message first arrived. I hopped down from the train, carrying my bag, and went to claim my horse. The new captain in the area, Captain McDonald, was unknown to me, and I had to ask a couple people for directions to the address they had given me. Austin, I could see, had been growing a lot since I'd been gone.

Before long I found myself outside a boarding house, by the look of it. I knocked on the door and was directed to a room at the end of a long hall. A deep voice told me to enter when I knocked on that door, and a short, blonde man with an impressive moustache rose to greet me when I entered.

"McKinnon?"

I nodded, and he pointed to a chair opposite a small, very cluttered desk.

"You knew Red." It wasn't a question. I said nothing and waited while he stared out a small window. He turned and looked at me again. "Red was bushwhacked. Shot from ambush while he was trailing a horse thief a little north of there. I'm assuming you want his murderer caught just about as bad as I do."

I leaned forward in my chair. "They shot him from ambush?"

McDonald looked down at his desk. His face was flushed, and the veins stood out in his forehead. He started to say something, then stopped. He nodded. "Bushwhacked. They found the spot where the horse thief laid down and waited for him."

The words spilled out of me. "I want him brought in just as bad as you, Cap'n, just like you said. Only I hope you're not too particular whether or not he comes in dead. I'd just as soon have him strapped over my pack horse as ridin' on his own horse." I sat back and waited for his answer. He'd have to send me back to West Texas if I couldn't have a free hand on this one.

McDonald looked out his window for a moment, then nodded slowly. He turned back to look at me. "You can defend yourself, McKinnon," he said. He shuffled a few papers on his desk. "You can defend yourself any way you need to. Does that answer your question?"

I nodded. "Is there anybody else workin' on this?" I asked. I thought for a moment. "Mike Stone? Can you assign Mike Stone?"

McDonald shook his head slowly. "I've got Stone working a case in North Texas right now." He shrugged. "Governor's request. Nothing I can do about it. If he frees up and you need the help, I'll assign him. Meanwhile, this is about tracking, and you're our best tracker."

He shoved the papers on his desk aside, then stood and spread out a map. I could see there were a few circles drawn in red on the map. I stood for a closer look. McDonald began pointing at the circles. "Lampasas—that's where the horses were stolen that Red was tracking." He pointed, one after the other, at three more circles. "Georgetown, Bartlett, Leander. They stole horses in all three places. Don't really know if they're connected, but we think so. Two of 'em had a new hand start working a week or so before the robberies. Then he disappeared a few days after. Not the same guy, though." He paused. "We haven't been able to follow the tracks after any of the robberies. Tracks seem to vanish into thin air. That's why I brought you in, McKinnon."

McDonald stopped and dropped into his chair. I leaned over the map and studied the four circles. They weren't really all that close to each other. "Can you tell if they were headed in the same direction? I mean, as far as you could track? Could they have been headed to the same place to meet up with somebody or sell the horses?"

McDonald shook his head in frustration. "Don't know. Couldn't track 'em far enough to say." Another thought struck him, and he got up and began to pace. "Here's something else. None of the horses have shown up since they were stolen. I mean, a lot of times, a horse will show up later, and you can tell the brand was altered with a running iron or something, but you know it's the same horse. Not with these guys, though. Not one horse has shown up since being stolen, and we've had some guys keeping an eye out for a while, all over the state."

I was feeling some of the frustration the cap'n was showing. I leaned back over the map and shook my head. "No tellin' where they're going to hit next, not with that map." I sat back down. "Anything else you can tell me? Do they steal the same kind of horses every time?"

McDonald started to shake his head no, then stopped. "They steal all different breeds, if that's what you mean. Only top dollar rides, though. These guys steal the best, most expensive horses wherever they go, and leave all the rest. That's if it's even the same guys doing all the robberies."

"I'm gonna assume it's the same gang doing all of it," I said, almost to myself. "If they prove me wrong, I'll just have to start over." I twirled my hat in my hand, trying to think of questions. "Did you find anything on Red, any notes?" I stopped, feeling embarrassed and not wanting to remember my friend as a dead man on a lonely trail. McDonald quickly shook his head no. I started to leave, then turned around with one last thought. "Is there a ranch, anywhere around any of these four spots," I said, pointing at the map, "that breeds really excellent horses? I mean, someplace maybe known as a ranch where you could go and get a top-notch horse?"

McDonald looked up, picking up on my idea. "You mean, someplace they might strike next?" I nodded. He looked at me blankly for a second, then shook his head. "I don't know, but I'll do some asking," he said. "Check back in with me sometime tomorrow, before you go."

I stood on the porch outside the boarding house and collected my thoughts for a minute. I didn't really know anybody in Austin, not with Mike Stone somewhere in North Texas. I decided to grab a bite and check into a hotel. It didn't sound like I was going to be in town for all that long.

Chapter Two
Longhorn Cave

Standing outside the hotel the next morning, I realized there were actually two people in Austin I knew and remembered. One was a lady everybody called Ma, who ran a boarding house down the road. I knew she served a mighty fine breakfast down there, and I liked to think I was one of her favorites. The other person was Mike Stone's wife, Sarah, who I'd met at the same time Mike did. I decided to make a call on both of them this morning, then swing by to see Captain McDonald again in the afternoon.

Ma swung the boarding house door open and clapped her hands together with delight. "Ash McKinnon! Get in here!" She ushered me through the door and herded me down the hallway, then introduced me to about a half-dozen people having what appeared to be the best breakfast I had ever seen. Of course, I had to allow for the fact that I'd been eating at what passed for a café in Langtry for the last several months.

I'd never been a boarder at Ma's place, but I had parked my feet under her table for several meals. She ladled up a heaping spoonful of scrambled eggs, then another, then about a half dozen sausages, and finally some toast and coffee. When I came up for air, she pushed a giant wedge of apple pie onto my plate. When she asked if I wanted more, I could only moan softly, loosen my belt, and lean back. She surveyed her handiwork in satisfaction.

"Tell us what you've been doing," she said.

I entertained them for about a half hour with stories about West Texas and Judge Roy Bean's court. Nobody there had heard of him, but they all vowed to stay clear of the judge if they ever found themselves in Langtry. Finally, I pushed my chair back.

"I've got to be going," I told Ma. "I need to stop in and see Sarah."

Ma beamed. Sarah had been a boarder at her place at one time. "Just a second," she told me. She disappeared into the kitchen, then returned with a napkin stuffed full of cookies. I reached into my pocket for some change, but she wouldn't hear of it.

"Just make sure you come and see me the next time you're in town," she said. I promised to do that, then mounted up and rode toward the land owned by Mike and Sarah Stone. They had jointly inherited the land in an odd twist of fate, and I knew they had made plans to build on it.

Sarah had her back to me, painting a new house that stood in the middle of a clearing on the creek that flowed past their land. Walnut Creek, if I remembered the name correctly. I started to call her name as I rode up, but she had already heard the creak of the saddle leather. She turned, then dropped the paintbrush into a can and sprinted toward me. I swung down, and she enveloped me a in a hug.

"Ash!" she exclaimed. "What a pleasant surprise! How long have you been here? What brought you to town? Are you hungry?"

I answered the last question first. I patted my stomach. "I've just been to Ma's place," I explained.

Sarah laughed, knowing what that meant. "Maybe you could use some coffee," she said, leading me into the house. I sat at the table, admiring the nice home they had built here, while she bustled around the small kitchen, making me a cup of coffee.

When she brought it to the table and sat down across from me, I took one more look around the house, then took a sip of the coffee. "I always said," I reminded her, "that Mike Stone is the luckiest devil I know."

Her laugh rang through the small house. "What about you, Ash? Haven't you found a girl yet?"

That Sarah. She always got right to the point. "I've been in Langtry, Texas, for months," I complained. "They don't have anything but a railroad, some miners, a couple salty old cowboys and a crazy judge. When was I supposed to find a girl?"

Sarah's laugh filled the house again. "OK, I guess I can see where that would be a problem," she admitted. "You're back in Austin, now, though. Maybe your luck will change."

"Not for long," I said, rather sadly. "I'll be off on a case soon. In fact, I wanted to see if you can tell me anything that might help. It's about Red Corbin's death."

The smile faded from her face instantly, and I kicked myself mentally for not easing into the subject a little more slowly. Sarah saw my expression and shook her head. "It's alright, Ash. You go ahead and tell me what I can do. Red stayed with us a few days before... well, before he went off on that last assignment."

I had been staring at the ground, but I lifted my eyes when she said he had stayed at their house. "Did he leave anything here?" I asked quickly. "Any papers or personal items or anything that might help me?"

She started to shake her head, then sat up suddenly. "There's an old cedar chest in the corner of the room where he slept. Let me look in there." She was on her feet in an instant and disappeared around the corner. I could hear a squeak or two from the other room as the lid of the chest opened and closed.

In a moment she reappeared, carrying an old vest. She held it out to me. "I've never seen this before. I'm sure it's not Mike's vest," she said. "It must have been Red's."

I nodded and held the vest up, thinking it might be about the size Red would have worn. I didn't recognize it, but then I hadn't seen Red in a year or more. I put it down in my lap and reached into the small pockets in front. The first was empty, but my hand emerged from the second pocket with two slips of paper. The first appeared to be a receipt for a pair of boots. I set that aside and opened the second piece of paper.

At first, it puzzled me, holding the paper out in the light from a window. It appeared to be the tracing of a man's boot print. I looked up at Sarah, who also looked puzzled. "It's a tracing of a boot print, I think," I told her. "I wonder if he saw this print more than once and thought it might have to do with the robberies."

On an impulse, I set the tracing down on the floor and stepped on the paper, comparing my boot print to the one on the paper. My boot print engulfed the print on the tracing. "Well," I said, "I do wear a size twelve boot." I gestured at Sarah. "You try."

She did as I asked. When she had placed her boot over the tracing on the paper, I could see that the one Red had traced was only slightly larger than Sarah's boot would leave. I sat back, puzzled.

"Either that is a woman's print, or a guy with a really small foot," I concluded. I folded the paper back up and put it in my pocket. "I'll keep this," I said. "Maybe it could help." I gestured at the vest. "I don't know what to do with that," I said slowly. "He didn't have any family that I ever heard him talk about."

Sarah folded the vest and placed it on the table, a few tears forming in the corners of her eyes. "I think the Rangers were his family," she said. "We'll keep it here for now."

I stood to go. "I need to get back to see Captain McDonald," I told her. "Make sure you give your best to Mike for me. I'm hoping the cap'n will assign Mike to this case when he finishes what he's doing."

Sarah smiled and gave me a hug. "I'll tell him," she said. "I guess I don't really need to tell you to be careful, but you remember what happened to Red. Keep your eyes open."

I mounted and walked my horse alongside the creek that ran past their new house, remembering an adventure that had ended right on the banks of this creek recently. I glanced back to see Sarah waving at me. I returned the wave, thinking that Mike Stone was probably still the luckiest devil I knew. Then I gave my buckskin a little kick in the ribs and took the road back to Austin.

Holt Jacobs rose early, made a quick breakfast, and started moving the horses down the trail toward the hideout. Longhorn Cave was tucked away to the east of the Colorado river, and a little southwest of the town of Burnet. Burnet was growing quite a bit because of the arrival of the railroad just last year, but it was still small enough for the little horse-stealing operation to remain a secret. Holt hadn't known about the cave previously. He'd been told about it when he was recruited into the gang. He had been fairly impressed to find out that Sam Bass had used it as a hideout at one time.

Leaving his camp just as light filtered through the trees, Holt worked his way south for several miles, then struck a path due west to the Colorado River. Losing the trail of the stolen horses in the Colorado river had been his contribution to the operation. Holt moved steadily, pulling over frequently to check his back-trail. Whenever he topped a rise, he stopped to scan the area in front of him as well. He didn't want to meet anybody or be seen by anybody. When it was mid-morning, he pulled off the trail and waited for evening before he began to move again. When he reached the Colorado, he made camp for the night.

Holt risked a small fire, heating his food and giving him a bit of warmth. He checked the horses and walked a small circle around his camp before settling down in his bedroll. When he didn't drift off to sleep immediately, he began reviewing in his head how he came to join up with this horse-stealing crew, and what his own plans would be for the future.

He had been approached by a man who identified himself only as Lance, several months earlier at the Sholz Garten saloon in Austin. Lance said he worked for a man who had money, connections, and a great plan to steal horses and sell them in another state. He said he'd been given Holt's name by somebody, but wouldn't say who. He said Holt could make maybe $250 a month. His job would be to first recruit two other men to help steal the horses and bring them to a hideout. Holt would get instructions by mail or a telegram at a hotel in Austin, telling him which ranches to rob and the type of horses to steal. He would never know the identity of the man who sent those messages. Holt, along with his recruits, would steal the horses and bring them to a hideout for a few days. After those few days, Holt, and only Holt, would meet Lance at a pre-arranged location and hand off the horses. His pay would come a week or two later at a pre-arranged pickup spot.

Holt was both interested and irritated with the proposal. Who was the guy in charge? That was his first question. Lance only shrugged. That, he said, would remain a mystery. Why the mystery? Lance shrugged again. They were all safer, he said, if all of them knew only as much as they needed to know. Those men he would recruit, for instance, would only have contact with Holt. They would get their instructions from him, and would know nothing about Lance or the man in charge of it all.

Lance met his insistence on learning more with a stone wall. Holt could take the offer as presented, or he could move on and Lance would find somebody else. They agreed to meet the next night at the Sholz Garten and Holt would give his answer. The money had been too good for him to pass on it, so he had agreed.

Now, several months later, he had recruited a couple of guys to help him. They weren't along on this particular job because he didn't need them—not when he was only stealing two horses. He preferred to work alone, anyway. They would wait at the Longhorn Cave when he got there. They were half-brothers named Ike and Slade, and they were the right combination of greedy and lazy. Greedy enough to get the job done, and lazy enough not to want more.

Holt, on the other hand, wanted more. He believed that if he could get rid of Lance and take his job, there would be a lot more money in it for him. His mind began working on the ways he could do that, and somewhere along the way he drifted off to sleep.

Moving at daybreak again, he led the horses to the edge of the river, then looked back at the hoofprints left behind them. This, he thought, is the one time he would have liked having his helpers along. Searching along the bank, he led the horses into the water, then down to a sizeable rock at the water's edge. He lifted the rock and placed the reins for his horse under it. Going back into the trees, he found a large branch and used it to cover the tracks, working his way from the tree line down to the water. He tossed the branch into the river when he was done, then mounted and splashed the horses through shallow water for a hundred yards.

After glancing around him in all directions, he swam the horses across the river, then splashed through the shallow water on the other side for another hundred yards. He then led the horses into cover on the far side, tethered them, and again covered the tracks. He would repeat this procedure twice more along the way as he worked south along the Colorado River.

Three days later, Holt approached Longhorn Cave from the west and south. As he travelled, he looked around him, realizing that this wouldn't work as a hideout for too much longer. More and more settlers had come into the area, and he and Ike and Slade depended on being able to graze the horses on empty land around the caves for several hours each day. It was vital for them to be able to do that unseen. Holt decided that was a problem for another day. Who knew what he would be doing in a few years?

Topping a rise, he could see Ike and Slade waiting at the usual spot near the cave. He handed off the horses, telling them to graze and water them. He proceeded into the cave, spread out his bedroll and proceeded to take a nap. He would have some work to do later today or tomorrow with a running iron, altering those brands. In another three days, he would take the horses to Lance for sale. This time, he intended to find out more about where those horses were going. There had to be more money for him in this operation.

I found Captain McDonald muttering to himself as he weeded through some paper on his desk. He left me shifting back and forth on a tiny and uncomfortable chair while he finished up what he was doing. Finally, he glanced up at me, mumbled to himself and reached for a paper or two at the edge of his desk. He glanced over at them, then handed them to me.

"Jessie Maitlin," he said. He leaned back and watched while I read the papers.

I'd never heard that name, but I settled down to read the papers he'd given me. The first page said that a woman named Jessie Maitlin owned a ranch near Belton, Texas, where she raised horses and grazed a few cows. I raised my eyebrows and looked at McDonald.

"Belton?" I asked.

"North of Austin, south of Waco," came the answer. "I hear she raises some pretty excellent stock, horse-wise."

It made sense. Maybe this ranch was a target. I turned to the second page, when I saw a hand-written note from this woman, saying she was worried about the number of horses being stolen, and asking for any help the Rangers could give her.

I started to hand the papers back to McDonald, but he waved them off.

"Keep 'em," he said shortly. "You're headed up there to look things over. Maybe you'll get lucky enough to be in the area when they strike next. You got any other ideas? Toss 'em out if you do."

I knitted my eyebrows together and leaned back in my uncomfortable chair. Nobody had ever said that thinkin' was my strongest point, but I was starting to enjoy this detective kind of work.

"Does she have any hired hands on the ranch?" I asked.

The captain thought about it for a second. "Maybe one," he answered finally. "I think they said she had one hand."

"So maybe she can pretend to hire me," I suggested. "I can be there for a week or two, check things out, maybe be on the spot if they try to steal her horses."

The captain reached for a blank piece of paper, picked up his pen, and scratched a note on the paper. "Give this to her," he said. He bent his head back down over some more papers on his desk and started scratching again with that pen. I realized our interview was over. I picked up my hat and left. I could ask somebody else how to get to the ranch.

Chapter Three
Jessie

I cantered north on the road toward Belton, my collar turned up against the cold wind beginning to blow in from the north. I began to regret my decision to start my trip immediately after my meeting with McDonald. I could, I thought, be holed up in a warm hotel room in Austin right now. I hunched down, leaned into the wind, and resolved to put in a couple more hours before making camp. At least, I told myself, I could make it to Belton and start working on the case sometime late tomorrow afternoon or early evening. I knew from my previous time in Central Texas that the weather could change at any time, with warm winds pushing up from the south.

I gave some thought to what I knew about these horse thieves. That was the disturbing part. I knew little—just that my friend Red had died trying to bring them in. I didn't really know how much help I needed. I had gone back to McDonald's office before leaving to ask if he could spare anybody to help me. He had told me to go up to Jessica Maitland's ranch and find out what I could. He promised to assign Mike Stone if he freed up. If not, he would bring Charlie Bass out from Langtry to help me. I was rooting for it to be Stone, but either one would be a welcome sight riding in.

I made a cold camp and started out early the next day. I decided to stop in at the saloon in Belton when I arrived there in the early evening. I needed some directions to the ranch, plus I didn't mind finding out what I could learn around town before showing up at the ranch with my letter from McDonald.

The bartender eyed me, slightly unfriendly, but not hostile, as I walked in. He came over when I took a seat at the bar. "You ain't been here before," he said.

"Nope." I didn't feel like telling him anything else. "Gimme a beer." He shrugged, filled a glass and shoved it down the counter to me.

About twenty minutes later, looking a little friendlier, he stopped in front of me. "Want 'nother?" he asked. I nodded, and he brought the glass over to me this time. Some people, I'd noticed, just naturally didn't trust strangers, but he seemed to be warming up.

He stayed put where he was for a minute, looking down the bar at the other customers. I decided to ask for directions. "Can you tell me how to get to the Lazy M ranch?" He stared at me blankly. "Maitlin Ranch," I explained.

"Oh." He pointed out the doors. "Take a right out those doors and go down the road mebbe three miles. Look for the sign on the left." He hesitated. "She ain't hirin', if'n that's what yore lookin' for."

I lowered my glass back to the bar. "How d'you know that?"

He shrugged. "Guy come in two, three days ago, asked me same thing you just asked. I was out on the front porch mebbe two hours later when he went by, headed in t'other direction. Didn't look none too happy."

"Oh," I said thoughtfully. "Well, maybe I'll try anyway. Maybe she'll like me better."

"Yeah," he said, a little doubtfully. "Well, that other guy did look a little shifty-eyed."

I chuckled, got up, and shoved some change across the bar. "I'll try not to let my eyes get too shifty." He laughed and waved as I left. I made a note to ask about the man who'd been looking for work. He could have been part of a plan to rob the ranch.

Jessie Maitlin sat on the porch of the ranch house, rocking gently in the evening chill, enjoying having the moment to rest. She kept an eye out for her younger brother, Kyle, who had been out checking on the livestock. It was just about time to move some of them to a fresh pasture, and they needed to start feeding hay. When Kyle came in, she would go inside and help her mother start dinner.

She reflected on how tired she was at the end of every day, at the tender age of twenty-four. It was no mystery how that had come about. She had wound up running the family ranch at the age of eighteen.

A sudden barking from the dog got her attention, and she stood quickly, shading her eyes against the setting sun. After a moment, she sighed and sat back down, not sure if she was amused or annoyed. The dog, a retriever/collie mix, had succeeded in running another squirrel up a tree. She was more than a little jumpy these days, worrying that her horse ranch was the target for another of the robberies she had been hearing about. They simply couldn't afford the loss.

Her eyes travelled from the corral in the yard out to the pastures beyond. She loved this place and knew she would never leave it, she just wished she didn't feel like everything was on her shoulders. Her parents had come to Texas in 1855, moving from Northern Georgia, lured by the inexpensive land and the promise it held. Her parents, she reflected, had given their lives to their family and this ranch. Those two things seemed inseparable.

Her father had marched off to war when she was not much more than a baby. Coming from another southern state, her parent's loyalty had been to the Confederacy, like most families around them, even though nobody owned slaves around here or were that caught up in arguments about state's rights. And so, her father had gone off to war in 1861. Ironically, he had survived the battles, and had come home with both arms and both legs intact. The war had killed him more slowly.

She shifted in the rocking chair and watched idly as some chickens clucked and scratched around in her mother's flower bed. She should have chased them away, but she didn't feel that energetic. Her thoughts returned to her father.

Harold Maitlin had marched away to war in May 1861, and after fighting in some small skirmishes and waiting out the winter of '61-'62, had been involved in the first day of fighting at Shiloh. It was malaria, not injuries, that kept him out of the second and third days. Ironically, malaria might have prevented him from being killed at Shiloh. The southern troops had been pushed back after the North received reinforcements, and her father's unit had been decimated on the second day. The malaria had taken his life, it just worked a lot more slowly.

Harold had, like a lot of troops, been exposed to miserable, damp weather and swarms of mosquitoes as they waited in their camps for the inevitable battle. He'd been suffering from fever and chills the first day at Shiloh, but he wasn't yet incapacitated. On the second day, he'd not been able to answer the call.

Removed to a sick tent, fellow victims of malaria had surrounded him, along with victims of typhoid and dysentery. Jessie knew that disease had killed more soldiers in the Civil War than had actual battles. Her father was among those who died an untimely death from disease.

Luckily for Harold and the family, the army had found enough quinine to give her father to stop the malaria at Shiloh. He had somewhat recovered over the next several weeks and had eventually returned to his unit. He had finished the war in General Joe Johnston's army, surrendering a few weeks after Appomattox. Jessie had been seven years old when he returned.

Her father had lived for another eleven years, though he suffered greatly from recurring bouts of the malaria. He fought through the fevers and weakness, usually managing to do a day's work before returning to his sickbed. She had seen, though, how the illness was wearing him down. She had done her best to go out to work beside him, learning everything she could about stock breeding, animal care, and ranching. The harsh winter of '75-'76 had left him with a lingering case of pneumonia, and he was too weak to fight it off. They lost him in the spring of 1876.

Jessie's mother had seemed lost for a year or more after her husband's death, leaving Jessie feeling isolated and alone. Her brother Kyle, born shortly after her father returned from war, had leaned on her for strength and comfort. Finally, her mother Iris had pulled herself together and resolved to make things work for her young family. Iris did most of the cooking and cleaning, and planting and harvesting a large vegetable garden. She looked after the chickens and milked the family cow every day. Kyle, now age seventeen, was becoming quite a help as well.

She heard hoofbeats and looked up to see Kyle riding up to the corral. He dismounted and led his horse into the corral, and Jessie went out to help him unsaddle and wiped down his gelding.

Kyle's horse was mainly of mustang blood, as were more than half the herd. Cowboys driving herds up the Chisholm trail to Kansas were their best customers, and the cowboys prized the toughness and endurance of the mustangs. Jessie knew the railroad was likely to change that before much longer, and she would have to figure out how to replace the loss of that business. That, she decided, was a worry for another day.

Putting an arm around Kyle's shoulders, she began walking with him to the house. The sound of hoofbeats stopped them, and Jessie turned around to see a large, rugged-looking man riding into the yard.

Jessie glanced, almost automatically, at the shotgun she had left resting against the corner of the porch. The string of robberies, compounded by the stranger who had appeared two days ago, looking for work, had left her on edge. Kyle sensed her tension and shuffled nervously.

The stranger followed her glance and lifted both hands disarmingly into the air. "Ash McKinnon, ma'am. Texas Rangers. Captain McDonald sent me." He reached slowly into his jacket and withdrew a folded-up piece of paper. Dismounting, he handed her the paper and removed his hat, shifting it between his hands while he waited for her to read it.

Jessie took the paper and read, glancing up at him when she had finished. "Well, Mr. McKinnon," she began.

He waved his hands. "Please ma'am, Ash. My daddy ain't here."

She relaxed, refolding the letter and looking at his disarming smile. There was a little more of a Southern accent in what he'd just said—maybe Kentucky or Tennessee, she thought. She wondered if he was able to turn that Southern accent on or off to relax people, or maybe throw them off balance. In any case, she tended to trust her instincts, and her instincts told her this one was a lot more trustworthy than the visitor from two days ago. Plus, he had the letter from the captain she had written to earlier.

The back door banged shut behind her, and Jessie turned to see her mother standing on the porch. Then she walked down the steps. She glanced at the stranger, then at Jessie. Jessie, recovering her manners, turned and held out her hand toward the new arrival. "Mother," she said, "this is Mr. Ash McKinnon, from the Rangers. My mother, Iris," she finished, waving back at her mother.

Iris stepped forward and took his proffered hand. Jessie noticed that it basically disappeared in the stranger's grip. "Mr. McKinnon," she began.

"Just Ash," he corrected.

"Well," said her mother, with a slow smile, "Just Ash, please join us for dinner. We have plenty," she assured him when she saw his doubtful expression.

"I'd be obliged, ma'am," he said. "Although plenty takes a powerful amount of food for a guy my size. I promise I'll go easy on you." Iris chuckled and turned toward the house. Ash fell in behind her.

Jessie hesitated only a moment, then followed them in, a smile beginning to spread across her face. That good-old Southern boy accent was becoming more pronounced by the minute.

I held myself back at dinner as best I could, although the food was delicious. I was pretty sure it would be bad manners to let my belt out a notch at the table. I stole a glance at Jessie every once in a while. She was downright beautiful—dark hair and dark eyes. She caught me looking one time and I'm pretty sure I blushed. "Ash," I said to myself, "don't go getting hooked on this girl. You've got a job to do. Next thing you know she'll be reeling you in and you'll just be floppin' around in the bottom of the boat."

Actually, the next thing I knew, Jessie had said something to me and I needed to answer. I searched my brain for the last thing she had said. Something about a man looking for work. My brain snapped back to the conversation with the bartender.

I nodded my head. "The bartender in town said someone had come through here, looking for work."

The surprise showed in her eyes. "The bartender knew about that?"

"I asked him for directions out to your ranch," I explained. "He figured I was comin' out here to look for work, because he said somebody else had come through and asked for directions just a couple days before. I guess that guy was headed out here next, looking for a job."

"OK, that makes sense." She seemed to relax a little, but I could see some strain and fatigue in her eyes. "Wait here," she said. "I want to show you something."

She returned with a piece of paper, which she pushed across the table to me. I picked it and saw that it was a drawing—a man's face. The detail was astonishing. I was looking at a man about my age, with hair thinning out a bit, a full beard, and eyes set slightly too close together.

"Wow," I said. "You can really draw." My eyes returned to the drawing, and I studied it a little longer. "I haven't seen this guy," I said, "but I'll send it to the captain. He might want to find somebody that can draw copies, then send them around to the other Rangers." I looked at it again, trying to memorize that face.

"Have there been other ranches, where maybe a stranger came to work and then the ranch got robbed?" she asked. I glanced up to see those pretty dark eyes locked in on me. I nodded slowly.

"There have been a couple," I said reluctantly. She seemed on edge and upset about this stuff already, and that answer wasn't going to make her feel any better about things.

I looked down at the table, trying to gather my thoughts. "You did exactly the right thing, not hiring him and making this drawing. He could be one of the gang." I cleared my throat and set the drawing down on the table. "I'm going to be here to help you," I finished. "Tell me more about the ranch and the horses. Start with where they are located."

Kyle cleared his throat and joined the conversation for the first time. He pointed toward the back wall of the house. "They're in the south pasture. It's the closest one we have to the house that has enough grass for them."

"Show me," I said. We stepped out the back door, and I could see the horses, maybe one hundred yards away. "How many?" I asked. They told me they had about seventy, including 3 foals. "This gang seems to go after the very best horses and then leave the rest. How many do you have that are what you would call your very best?"

They looked to Jessie for that answer, and she took her time, thinking it over. "I would say ten," she answered. "We have one stallion with Arabian bloodlines. He has a lot of speed. So, we have that stallion, maybe six of the best mares, and three colts that they might go after. What do you want us to do?"

I looked at a small, enclosed pasture off to one side. It was more like a big corral, but it looked to be large enough for ten horses, from what I could see in the fading light. "What's that pasture for? If we threw out some hay, could you graze the ten horses in there, closer to the house?"

Kyle started moving, trotting off the back porch. "We call it the birthing pasture," he said over his shoulder. "I'll throw some hay out there and bring the horses in before it gets too dark."

I looked at some trees bordering the birthing pasture on the west side. "I'll get my bedroll," I said. "I'll be sleeping over in those trees."

Jessie came in the back door of the house, carrying a lantern. It had taken both of them, working together, to cut out the horses they needed and bring them to the birthing pasture, while Kyle had finished throwing out the hay before darkness had completely settled in. She had gone back out to bring water and a little food to Ash.

She saw a glow of lantern light coming from the kitchen as she walked back to the house. She found her mother washing the dishes from dinner. Jessie put her lantern down and picked up a towel to help.

Iris turned her head as Jessie came in. "Is he settled down out there?" She looked out the window. "I hope it won't be too cold. What if it starts raining on him?"

Jessie took the questions one at a time. "He knows the way to the back porch if it rains. And I told him to come in and throw his bedroll down in the living room, next to the fireplace, if it gets too cold." She paused. "I have a feeling it would have to get really cold before he would come in, though."

Iris finished washing the dishes and picked up a towel to dry her hands. "I think he's a good man," she said. "He's kind of... ruggedly handsome, don't you think?"

Jessie felt herself blushing slightly and looked up to see her mother's amused smile. She smiled despite herself. "Yes," she said after a moment. "I guess that's a pretty good description of him. I'm glad he's here."

Chapter Four
Horse Handoff

Holt Jacobs tore open the envelope in the Austin hotel lobby, surveying his latest instructions. The usual furrow of frustration on his forehead was even more pronounced than usual. He had two reasons for being irritated with this latest set of instructions.

First, the directions were very vague. Jacobs had long suspected that The Boss had somebody that travelled to the target ranches and hired on for a week or two prior to the robbery. When the man wasn't able to hire on, the instructions got a lot more vague on which horses to take. This note said to visit the Lazy M Ranch near Belton. So far, so good. Then it just directed him to take the stallion and three or four of the best-looking mares. Holt blew out a snort of exasperation. Noticing that he had drawn a few curious stares, he moved out to the street.

Having to look things over and choose the horses would require him to hang out in the area for an extra day or two, increasing his chances of getting caught. And if they weren't happy with the horses he took, they would blame it on him.

The second thing that bothered him was that the note said he had to make this happen within the next week or so. He had noticed that he was being given less and less time to pull off these robberies. Plus, he had planned to shadow Lance this time when he went to transport the horses for sale. Following the trail of the stolen horses was important to him. It was the first step in his plan—it would help him get a bigger share of the profits. Holt suspected they were being shipped by rail, which suggested that there was another guy on the robbery payroll, working for the railroad. He at least needed to find out who that was.

Holt folded up the note, put it in his pocket and unhitched his horse from the rail. He paused before stepping into the saddle, one hand on the pommel of his saddle. He had to decide what to do about the timing problem he had now. He couldn't follow Lance and get back in time to take one of his helpers to Belton and pull off the robbery. He stepped into the saddle and turned his horse out into the street. Holt knew what he would do. He would follow Lance first, then come back for the Lazy M robbery. He could make some excuse for the delay. They needed him too much to get rid of him for one late job.

Holt tied the rope from one of the stolen horses to his saddle horn. It was time to move the two horses he had stolen several days ago. It was barely light, but he always preferred to move the horses early. Looking behind him, he could see one of his men, Slade, doing the same with the other horse. Ike lounged against a tree, hands in his pockets, watching them. Holt had given up trying to figure out which one of them irritated him more. It was a tie, he decided.

"You," he said, pointing at Ike, "be ready to head out with me when I get back. Maybe in a couple days. I expect to have another job by then."

Ike removed a twig from his mouth, leaned over and spit, then nodded. He resumed leaning against the tree.

Holt shook his head and mounted up. He'd wanted people who were too lazy to get ideas about more money, so he'd gotten what he asked for. He kicked his horse in the ribs and moved out. The meeting point with Lance was north of Austin. He could be there tomorrow. Then he planned to send Slade back to the cave to wait. Meanwhile, Holt would go to see what he could find out about where these horses wound up after he handed them off to Lance.

Two days later, Holt met up with Lance for the handoff of the horses. The meeting spot was well hidden from any roads or trails, but Holt could always find it by moving north from the cave until he reached the Lampasas River. It was just a short distance east from there. Holt watched silently while Lance looked the horses over, grunted with what might have been approval, and tied a rope from each horse to his own. Occasionally, Holt had seen him come with a helper to transfer the horses, but today he was alone.

"Want some help?" Holt offered, sensing an opportunity.

Lance half-turned, sent a withering stare in Holt's direction and shook his head. "Nope." He stepped into the saddle and began leading both horses away. "You'll get paid in the usual way," was his only other comment. He led the horses off in an easterly direction, glancing back once in a while to be sure there was no pursuit.

Holt shrugged and watched him ride away. He hadn't really expected to be invited along. Lance had been secretive, just like the man running the show, who never tipped his hand. Holt turned and waved a hand at Slade. "You can go back to the cave," he said. "I'm gonna go and see if we have any instructions on the next job. I'll meet you and Ike in a couple days."

Holt watched for a few minutes while Slade rode back toward the south, then wasted no further time in striking Lance's trail. Lance had followed a narrow game trail, winding through small stands of oak trees. Holt stayed out of sight, but had no trouble following tracks left by three horses. After two hours had elapsed, he found himself climbing a small rise. Holt dismounted and led his horse up to the top of the rise, where he glanced cautiously over the top. He could see Lance riding down to the bottom of a sloping meadow, where he turned onto a road and headed for a town, not too far in the distance.

Holt took a seat at the top of the rise. He was pretty sure the town in the distance was Temple. He looked speculatively at the railroad tracks running through the town and leading off to the north.

His job now was to find out who the contact at the railroad was, and, if possible, to find out where the horses were being shipped.

After about ten minutes, Holt rose and trotted his horse down the slope and took the road to the edge of the town. He hitched his horse to a rail on the main street, pulled his hat down low over his forehead, and began to saunter toward the railroad station. He moved methodically, checking both sides of the street as he worked in toward the center of town.

As he neared the station, he saw the two stolen horses hitched across the street from the railroad and a few yards to the south of it. Holt retreated a block and sat down on a bench with his hat pulled low, awaiting developments.

It turned out he didn't have to wait long. After a few minutes, Lance emerged from the station house, accompanied by a burly man with an impressive black moustache. They walked over to the horses and exchanged a few words. Lance passed some money to the other man and walked away. The second man stood for just a moment, then unhitched the horses and led them to a corral inside the railroad yard, where he handed the reins to a stock handler, then returned to the station.

Holt remained on the bench as Lance walked away in the other direction on the street. Holt watched him until he ducked into a saloon. He returned his attention to the railroad yard, where the two horses had been turned out into a corral, apparently awaiting a train to take them away. He watched the handler speculatively as the man turned away from the corral and shuffled back to his post at the edge of the yard.

Taking a chance, Holt rose and sauntered over to the handler, who appeared to be no older than about twenty. He looked extremely bored, casting a curious glance in Holt's direction as he approached. Holt came to a stop beside him, took off his hat and ran his hand through his hair. He pointed at the two stolen horses in the corral.

"Nice horses," he offered.

The youngster cast a bored glance toward the horses. "I reckon," was all he had to say.

"I was thinkin' about working for the railroad," Holt said. "Do you like doing this?"

The young man snorted and shook his head vigorously from side to side. "Hate it. Couldn't get no proper job, cowboyin' for a ranch, so I took this. Still lookin' for something else, though."

Holt nodded and took a step or two away. Then he turned and threw a casual question over his shoulder. "Where are these horses going, anyway?"

The handler paused and glanced up at the horses. "The train stops at various places in the Nation and Kansas and Missouri," he said. "Those two are goin' to Parsons, Kansas." Seeing the ticket agent with the moustache emerge from the station, he made a show of picking up a broom and sweeping off the steps leading up to the station doors. Holt tipped his hat and retreated quickly out to the street.

Holt reached the street and placed his hat down low over his forehead again. He had found out everything he had come here to learn, but he felt like pushing his luck. Anything he could learn about Lance could work to his advantage, somewhere down the road. He decided to return to his seat on the bench and watch to see what Lance would do after he emerged from the saloon.

His patience was rewarded after about a half hour. Lance emerged from the saloon, staggering slightly, wove his way down the street to his horse and climbed aboard. Holt pulled his hat down a little farther as Lance trotted past on his way out of town. Feeling bolder after seeing the condition of his quarry, Holt hustled down the street to his horse and began trailing.

Lance struck a trail to the south, along the main road toward Austin. Not surprised, Holt followed at a comfortable distance. When the other man picked up the pace, Holt followed suit. He glanced overhead. It was a little before noon. He believed that Lance lived in Austin. Maybe he was trying to get there before dark.

After about four hours of pushing the horses hard, Lance entered a town and cantered down the main street, then hitched his horse to the rail. Holt pulled up at the edge of town, assuming that Lance had found another saloon on his way home. He leaned over to read the town name on the sign to his right. He was in Granger, Texas. Holt watched as Lance strolled casually up and down the street, looking over one business in particular. Holt couldn't quite make out what he was looking at. Finally, Lance mounted the steps and went inside one store.

Moving a short way down the street, Holt squinted against the sun and slowly read the sign on the storefront Lance had been eyeballing. His eyes widened when he saw the name: "First Bank of Granger." Being an old, experienced bank robber himself, he was immediately suspicious. He wondered if Lance was holding up the bank right now. Holt relaxed slightly as Lance came back out of the building he'd entered just a few minutes before. Lance walked casually up and down the street, then seemed to walk down the path between two of the buildings, no doubt checking for any entrance or exit to the bank from the rear.

Now sure of what he was seeing developing, Holt watched until he saw Lance enter a boarding house. After about twenty minutes, he emerged from the boarding house and walked down to a diner. Holt turned his horse and rode out of town, looking for a spot to make a cold camp. He felt sure Lance planned to rob that bank tomorrow, and he knew how to take advantage of it. A small smile broke out on his face as he considered the possibilities.

I sat on the back porch of Jessie's house, sipping the coffee she had brought me while I looked at the drawing she had made of the man who had tried to find work at her ranch. The face was distinct; the nose was broad and flat, while the eyes seemed set unusually close together. I folded it back up and put it in my pocket, then walked out to the corral that now contained the best horses on this ranch. I called it a corral at this point. The Maitlins called it the birthing pasture, but they knew what I was talking about. I leaned against the rails, sipping slowly from my coffee cup.

A common pattern of these robberies was that they stole only a few of the horses, and those few were the best on the ranch. They left horses prized by most cowboys alone, those being mustangs or other horses that had a lot of endurance and wouldn't cost too much. I knew how that worked. My mustang wasn't gonna win any races.

Jessie showed up beside me, and it caught me by surprise. I felt pretty self-conscious as I began to ask a question, stuttered a bit, then dug in my heels and tried again. If she noticed how tongue-tied I was, she was nice enough to ignore it. I steadied myself down and motioned toward the horses with my coffee cup.

"Who buys these horses?" I asked. "I don't think most cowboys could come up with money for those."

Jessie nodded in agreement. "You're right," she said. "My stallion has Arabian blood, and I charge more for these than I do for the ones most cowboys buy." She stopped to think for a minute. "I sell some of these to other horse breeders. I've had a few people buy them to ship back east for racing. Quarter horse racing," she clarified. "Most of my money comes from other horses I'm selling to people for cattle drives. Mainly I breed these because my dad and I loved good horses."

I nodded absently, staring out at that Arabian stallion in the corral, and the foals that came from him. I started to take another sip of coffee, then looked at the bottom of the cup in surprise when I came up empty.

Jessie chuckled and took the cup. "I'll get you another," she said.

"Much obliged," I told her. "The coffee I've been making for myself on the trail is just shocking bad." I shook my head at the memory. "My coffee pot is about twenty-five years old. My granddaddy gave it to me. Maybe that's the problem."

Jessie laughed and followed my gaze around the corral. Then she asked the question I had been thinking about. "Do you think the thieves have moved on because I didn't hire the man they sent around here?"

I looked over in surprise at how we'd thought the same thing. A plan was shaping up in my mind, though. "Could be," I answered. I couldn't read the expression in her eyes. I hoped I was seeing relief at not getting robbed and disappointment that I might move on. I was getting lost in those eyes, so I looked back out at the horses right quick.

I drummed my fingertips on the top of the rail. "Is there anybody else around here who raises some pretty pricey horses, maybe a little like what you've got out there? Somebody who might have horses these guys would want to steal?"

She thought for a bit, then nodded slowly. "There's somebody about a half-day's ride south of here. He bought a colt from me about three years ago, and he's using that horse as a sire now. He got some pretty good mares from a brother in Kentucky." She looked over at me. "Are you wanting to move on down the road and look there?"

This time I was pretty sure I heard a little disappointment in her voice. That's what I wanted to think, anyway. I shook my head back and forth. "Not leavin' for good," I assured her. "I might ride down there with this picture you drew and see if the same guy tried to hire on down at that place. First, though, I'll check around here. Really thorough, to see if anybody's been skulkin' around out there."

A smile crossed her face briefly. "OK, Ash. You look for those skulkers and I'll make you some breakfast. Mom would shoot me if I let you ride away from here hungry."

I circled the corral/birthing pasture on foot first, looking for boot prints all the way around the structure. I could only find the tracks I had made this morning, along with a few from Jessie, also this morning, and a couple others I knew must have been made by Jessie's brother Kyle last night.

I mounted up and began moving around in widening circles, looking especially for signs in the trees on the left of people passing through on horseback—broken twigs, tracks, and things such as that. In the pasture in back of the corral, there were too many horse tracks to help me. I sat my horse for a moment, studying the land around

Jessie's house. I felt sure that anybody intent on theft would have to pass through the trees on the west side where I had slept last night. There just wasn't enough cover if they came from any other direction.

Satisfied that nobody had tried to sneak up on the ranch and the horses last night, I headed on in for breakfast. Jessie's mom wouldn't need to worry about me riding away hungry. They piled my plate to the rafters and I could barely finish it. Finally, I sat back and thanked them for the breakfast.

Iris lifted a plate of biscuits and started to pass them in my direction. I held up my hand and waved the biscuits off. "They're delicious," I told her, "but I'm worried about my horse. He could get hurt trying to give me a ride if I eat any more."

Jessie came outside with me as I tossed my bag on the horse and led him around to the front of the house. She stopped me with a hand on my sleeve as I mounted up. "Come with me," she said.

I followed her around the corner of the corral where I saw a big chestnut gelding hitched to the rail. I walked over to the horse, admiring the lines and the size of him. He was at least sixteen hands. I looked at her questioningly. "Is he from your Arabian stallion?" I asked.

Jessie nodded. "My Arabian stallion and one of my mustang mares," she answered. "He has good speed and a lot of endurance. Why don't you give him a try? You may need him to catch the guy you're after."

I took one more look at the chestnut, then I unhitched him and led him over, switched saddles and prepared to mount up. Jessie stopped me and gave me a brief hug. "Be careful," she said. I grinned ear-to-ear and mounted the chestnut. I could feel that hug all the way down to my toes.

Chapter Five
No Honor Among Thieves

Holt rose early the next morning, having a cup of coffee for breakfast along with a little beef jerky. Not that he was in a hurry, he reflected, he just couldn't afford to have Lance see him in town this morning. After he had paced impatiently for at least a couple of hours, he pulled the watch from his pocket and checked it for about the tenth time. He saw that he had only about fifteen minutes before the bank opened, so he quickly saddled his horse and began moving toward town.

Pausing frequently to check his pocket watch, Holt arrived in town exactly at opening time for the bank—nine o'clock. He rode across to the north side of town, hat pulled low over his forehead. He noted only one horse hitched to the rail outside the bank, and he was pretty sure he had seen it there yesterday. It probably belonged to the owner or manager of the bank.

Arriving at his chosen spot on the north side of town, he tethered his horse as far away from the bank as he could while he could still see what was happening down there. He made a show of tightening the girth on the saddle, checking his horse's hooves, and trying to look preoccupied with anything other than watching the bank.

Just as he was feeling like he needed to move his horse and get out of town, he saw Lance leave the boarding house. Holt mounted but stayed where he was, watching. Lance unhitched his horse and led it across the street where he hitched it to the rail outside the bank. He reached into his saddlebag and removed what appeared to be a burlap sack. Looking both ways, he climbed the steps to the bank.

Holt had seen what he needed to see. He turned his horse and left town, heading to the north. Holt was taking a bit of a chance, but he intended to ride north until he reached the turnoff that would lead to the place where he always met with Lance to hand off the stolen horses. He felt sure that's where Lance would go to shake pursuit. Besides, he couldn't take the chance of following Lance and being overtaken by a posse on his trail. He kicked his mare in the ribs and picked up the pace.

Pulling off the trail in a stand of burr oak trees, just short of the Lampasas River, Holt dismounted, tethered his horse and sat down to wait. Leaning against a tree and taking a swig of water from his canteen, he figured he had little to lose if Lance didn't come this way. He could still make the robbery at the Lazy M. He could come back once in a while to keep an eye on Lance, but Lance might not know much more than how to arrange the shipment of the horses. The one with the mustache at the railroad. That was the man with the next piece of information. If Lance proved to be a dead end, he would watch the railroad man for a while. At the end of this trail, Holt needed to know who was sending his orders—who was he stealing the horses for? That man was making a lot of money. And depending on who he was, Holt had a feeling that man could be blackmailed.

Patience was rewarded about forty-five minutes later when Holt heard hooves pounding toward him. He rose and peered through the trees as Lance galloped past him, slowing the horse as he splashed into the river. He reined the horse over to the left, working his way to the west, leaving no tracks for the posse that was sure to be following. Holt watched as Lance stayed in the water for about two hundred yards, then abruptly guided the horse out of the river and into the trees. Lance returned briefly with a tree branch, brushed dirt over his tracks, then disappeared again.

Holt was in no hurry to follow, still feeling confident he knew where Lance was headed. Holt untethered his horse and led it on foot, deeper into the trees and away from the trail. When he reached a deep thicket well back from both the trail and the river, he tethered the horse securely and made his way back, on foot, to his original vantage point. Unsatisfied with the view he had of the trail and the river, he selected a large oak with a low-hanging limb and climbed up the tree. Finding a wide, level limb, he settled in, leaning back against the trunk, and resumed watching the trail.

It was another two hours, by the time on Holt's pocket watch, before a posse showed up on the trail. Led by a man with a badge Holt assumed to be the sheriff of Granger, it was a rag-tag bunch of five men, including one man who was barely hanging on to his horse. Holt chuckled under his breath, knowing the sheriff had probably had to make a sweep of the saloon to get himself a posse.

The group reached the bank of the Lampasas River and milled about uncertainly on the edge. The sheriff moved his horse uncertainly up and down the bank, then finally swam his horse across the river. The posse followed and spread out on the opposite bank, moving up and down, trying to find a trail. After a few minutes, the group moved off down the trail, away from the river, scouting for signs. Holt stayed where he was, certain they would return.

They were back just a few minutes later, re-crossing the river and splitting up to scour the bank for signs in both directions. Holt watched with interest as the sheriff and another man reached the place where Lance had left the river and moved into the trees. They passed the spot and moved on. After another thirty minutes of trying to pick up Lance's trail, they regrouped where the road met the river. After a few minutes of heated discussion, the sheriff led the group back toward Granger.

Holt waited for only a few minutes after the posse moved out of sight before shinnying back down the tree and starting for his horse. It was only about noon, and Lance might or might not hole up for the rest of the day at their meeting place. Things would get a little more difficult if he moved on from there today.

Holt mounted up and moved north to a point near the river bank, then moved west, casting back and forth until he struck the narrow game trail he was looking for. He held the horse to a walk, noting a familiar landmark here and there along the trail. After about an hour, he dismounted and led his horse forward.

After another ten minutes on foot, he hitched the horse one more time and crept forward, moving from tree to tree, watching the small clearing in front of him. He could see Lance seated on the ground, feeding small branches into a fire he had built. Holt smiled when he saw the whiskey bottle in Lance's right hand. Judging by the number of swigs the man was taking, this was going to be easy. He stayed behind a tree and watched as Lance finished the bottle and dropped it on the ground. After a few more minutes he flopped onto the ground, rolled over, and began snoring.

Not bothering to step quietly, Holt drew his gun, reversed his grip, and moved into the clearing. When Lance stirred and rose, Holt struck him soundly across the forehead with his gun barrel. Lance slumped soundlessly back to the ground. Holt moved across the clearing and lifted the saddlebag from the ground at the far edge of the clearing. Flipping it open, he reached inside and lifted the bundle of bank notes and the small bag of coins.

Holt sat down and quickly counted the take from the bank robbery, then snorted in disappointment. The total came to only $634. Holt shook his head and stuffed the money into the pocket of his jacket. No wonder the posse had quit so easily. He reached back into the bag, then changed his mind and dumped the contents out onto the ground. Sorting through a random collection of ammunition, canteen, and bits of food, he stopped and picked up a small notebook. He glanced over his shoulder at Lance, who hadn't stirred.

He returned his attention to the notebook and hastily shuffled through the pages, ripping several of them as he went. He found his own name in there, along with the hotel address Lance used to communicate with him. He stopped at the next name he found: A. Pendleton. There was an address listed in Temple. He stuffed the notebook into his pocket and turned to go.

Holt stopped at the edge of the clearing, gun in hand, and briefly considered killing Lance. After a moment, he rejected the idea. He still needed Lance to hand off the horses and keep the operation going. His best bet now was to pay Pendleton a visit. Or maybe he could break into Pendleton's house first. Maybe he could find something that would tell him who was buying those horses up north. If he was really lucky, maybe he could find out who was giving the orders.

Mike Stone rode slowly toward the Denton county jail, his prisoner tied to the saddle and trailing on the horse behind him. It was the end of a very long pursuit, and he was looking forward to handing over the prisoner. Horace Beane, or "Three Finger Beane" as he was more commonly known, had left a trail of theft and shootings across half the state. Stone had never heard the term "pecos" as anything but a reference to the West Texas river until he had started working this case. Now, unfortunately, he knew what it meant. Beane had murdered two men, thrown them in the Pecos River, and fled. Apparently when a man was murdered and thrown in the Pecos River, it was called a "pecos". Most recently, Stone had caught up with Three Finger trying to rustle cattle from a herd headed north on the Chisholm Trail.

Reaching the county jail, Stone handed the prisoner over without ceremony. He was looking for a room at a boarding house and then a café, in that order. He found a room, stopped just long enough at the telegraph office to send a telegram to his captain in Austin, and crossed the street to a café. After living on beef and beans for the last three weeks, he was hoping for anything else for dinner. Seeing nothing but beef on the menu, he gave up and ordered a steak.

After breakfast at the same café in the morning, he crossed the street to check for a reply to his telegram from the night before. To his surprise, he found a long telegram waiting for him. He left the telegraph office, parked himself on a bench he saw outside, and settled down to read what his captain had to say.

Captain McDonald began by congratulating him on the capture of Three Finger Beane. The governor, he assured Stone, would be pleased. McDonald went on to tell him that he needed to partner with Ash McKinnon on a case involving a ring of horse thieves. A smile crossed Stone's face; he and McKinnon had worked a cattle drive, then joined the Rangers at the same time. The smile faded when he was reminded that they had killed his friend Red Corbin while trailing one of the thieves.

Stone stood up, paced up and down for a few minutes, then settled back down to read the rest of the telegram. The horses being stolen were only the most expensive ones to be found on whatever ranch was being robbed. Several had Arabian blood, and they had found none so far in Central Texas where the robberies had all taken place. They had attached a description of several of the horses. McDonald advised him to return on the train to Austin, where he could talk with the captain further. McKinnon, he was told, was looking for the thieves in the area of Belton, Texas.

Stone stood and moved down to the boarding house to pay his bill. As he stepped out of the boarding house, he stopped and looked at the telegram again. Several of the horses, it said, had Arabian blood. He drifted to unhitch his horse, then changed his mind and crossed to the telegraph office again. He sent off a note to McDonald, telling him he wanted to check something there in North Texas concerning the ring of horse thieves before coming to Austin.

Stone mounted and rode north and slightly east, angling over toward the Chisholm Trail. He had seen a lot of impromptu horse race tracks set up along the trail during his drive a few years ago. And, from time to time, he had seen a few of them more recently, since he'd begun working as a Texas Ranger. Mostly, they seemed pretty harmless. He had ridden over to watch one of them during the cattle drive when the herd had stopped for a day in the Indian Territory.

A lot of the cowhands on the drives liked to race their horses. Usually there was a little betting going on—sometimes more than a little. The thought that had crossed his mind was that maybe the horse thieves were selling the stolen horses to men who were winning money at the race sites that had sprung up along the trail. Maybe that's where a few of them went, anyway. Maybe, he thought, if the horses were good enough, they could be sold for racing back east.

Cantering north and east on the road out of Denton, Stone struck the Chisholm Trail and followed it north for a few miles, remembering a crudely constructed racetrack he had visited a few years ago, hopeful it was still there. He held to the western edge of the trail. He was rewarded just a few miles later when he saw a carved wooden sign: "Shady Grove Races," it announced. Written below in letters he could barely make out, it said, "Must bet at least 25 cents. No more than $2 allowed".

Stone followed a faint, worn trail off to the west, nodding briefly at a couple of cowboys who passed in the opposite direction. He guessed they were returning to a herd somewhere up the trail. Trail bosses usually had a pretty tight schedule, but they knew they had to let the boys blow off a little steam once in a while.

After a few more minutes, he could follow his ears to the racetrack. The sound of pounding hooves and shouts grew louder until he rounded a bend and saw one hundred or so people standing around a dusty oval, with a tent pitched here and there. Stone knew they would be taking bets and selling beer in those tents.

He rode up to the track and hitched his horse at a rail, ignoring men shouting at him from the tents. He spotted a makeshift corral to one side where he assumed they kept the horses before and after the races. He stopped briefly and scanned the telegram—there were a few of the stolen horses described there. He stuffed the telegram back into his pocket after a brief read and headed to the corral. Stone figured his best bet was to look for an altered brand, rather than hoping to be lucky enough to find one of the few horses mentioned in the telegram.

Moving into the corral, he moved among the horses, hoping he looked like a serious bettor trying to choose the next horse to risk his money on. He patted a few before moving back to check a few of the brands. A black gelding caught his eye. It was a nicely built horse; Stone was guessing he was fast. The brand had really caught his attention. It was a circle R brand, but it looked like the brand had been something else before. Somebody had worked this one with a running iron.

Stone noticed motion at the corner of his eye. He turned to see a man advancing toward him out of the crowd. His face looked like an angry thundercloud. Stone turned slightly to face him. As he did, the man caught sight of the badge on his chest, turned, and disappeared into the crowd.

Stone moved after him immediately. He plunged into the crowd, glimpsing briefly the man heading toward a tent at the far end of the oval. He tried to follow, but men stood or moved into his way, moving only slowly as he pushed his way through. Emerging from a knot of people, he couldn't see the man anywhere.

Stone ran toward the tent where he had last seen the man headed, then ran to the entrance, shoved the flaps aside, and plunged into the tent. Bettors were lined up in front of two tables, shouting and waving money. Stone surveyed the crowd quickly, then checked under the tables. There was no sign of the man he'd pursued into the tent. His shoulders slumped in frustration. Then he noticed a flap at the back of the tent. He ran to the back and pushed through the flap. He saw nothing initially, then movement off to his left caught his eye. His quarry was sprinting into the corral.

Frustrated that he hadn't stayed with the horse, Stone ran toward the corral where he saw the man leap onto the black gelding and bolt out of the corral bareback as another man swung the gate open. Shouting for the man to stop, Stone knew the words were futile as soon as they left his mouth. He sprinted for his horse and jumped aboard.

Spurring his horse onto the trail, he gave chase. Within a few minutes, he knew there was no point in keeping up the pursuit. The black gelding had undoubtedly been stolen for his speed and racing ability. The dust trail Stone was following became less and less visible. It mingled with whatever tracks had been left with dozens of other tracks. There was nothing to follow. He slowed his horse to a stop, shaking his head in anger and frustration.

Finally, Stone reined his horse around to return to the racetrack. He would question the guy who had held the gate, if he could find him. He could look for any other horses with altered brands. He didn't hold out a lot of hope.

Chapter Six
Scout's Trail

My new chestnut gelding, which wasn't my horse, I had to remind myself, moved with a long, even stride. I urged him into a gallop for a few minutes, then brought him back down to a canter and began wondering how much it would cost to buy this horse. He covered the ground effortlessly, and he could really run. He hadn't even been one of the ten horses Jessie had brought into the corral in back of the house. I realized how big a target her ranch could be for the thieves.

I rode into Belton and kept going. I estimated it was a little past noon when I saw the place I was looking for. A sign on the trail said "Atherton". There was a ramshackle fence out front, and a small ranch house sat at the edge of a pasture. I could see a pasture behind, with maybe thirty horses and seventy head of cattle. There was a small bunkhouse at the edge of the pasture. A small, wiry man with a weather-beaten face and permanent crows' feet etched around his eyes approached me, neither welcoming nor unwelcoming as he stopped and looked me over.

I pushed my jacket to the side and let him see the badge hanging from my shirt pocket. He glanced at it and nodded, his expression never changing. He hooked his thumbs into his pants pockets and waited for me to say something.

I swung down from the horse, stretched for a minute, then fished in my pocket for the drawing that Jessie had given me. "McKinnon," I said, pointing a thumb at my chest.

His lips barely moved when he said, "Call me Zeb." He held his hand out for the drawing, and I could see the recognition in his eyes when he looked at it. He studied it for a few more seconds, then handed it back to me. "Yep, he was here, if'n that's what yore wantin' to ask me," he said.

I felt my heartbeat pick up the pace a little. "When?" I asked.

"Yestiddy," came the reply. "He were lookin' for work, but I told him I didn't have nothin' for him. It was gettin' on toward dark when he come, so I let 'em stay over yonder in the bunkhouse for the night. He rode outta here at daybreak."

My hopes rose and fell as I listened. I'd missed him by only a few hours. I folded up the drawing, pushed it back in my pocket and rocked back on my heels, trying to figure out what to do now.

Zeb watched me through shrewd eyes. He cleared his throat and spit, then looked at my horse and nodded in appreciation. He looked back at me. "Is he a bad'un?" he asked.

I nodded my head slowly. "Could be," I said. "Might be part of a crew that's been stealing top-notch horseflesh around these parts for the last several months. Any idea where he went when he left here?"

Zeb shook his head. "Said he was lookin' to buy some good harrses." Zeb snorted and shook his head again. "I guess my horses wasn't good 'nough for him." He thought it over, then added grudgingly: "maybe I was lucky. I guess he were plannin' to steal the harrses." He thought a minute longer. "I tole him about the Maitlin ranch." He pointed up north, where I'd come from. "He didn't go thataway when he hauled outta here, though." He pointed to the south. "He went thataway."

I looked down the trail to the south. "Any idea where he would go down that way?"

Zeb shook his head again. "Don't know any harrses better'n mine that he'd want to buy. Or steal. I tole him he could bunk up here again if'n he passes back through in the next couple days, though."

I saw a little hope. "Can I stick around here today, maybe stay over in the bunkhouse, see if he comes back through here in the next day or so?" Zeb looked a tad bit doubtful, so I sweetened the pot. "I could do some work for ya."

Zeb's eyes brightened up, and he hatched a small smile for the first time. He looked me up and down. "I reckon a boy yore size could split a powerful amount of wood, if'n he put his mind to it." He pointed toward an enormous pile of logs, off to the side of the house.

I looked at the woodpile, blew out a miserable breath, then nodded my head up and down in agreement. My big mouth got me in trouble when I was eatin' and when I was talkin'. Other than that, I didn't have any trouble with it, far as I could tell. I led the chestnut over to the corral and hitched him to the rail. Then I went over to the woodpile, picked up the ax, and started chopping.

Morning found me sore and no closer to finding the guy in Jessie's drawing. He hadn't returned, and I couldn't hang around here anymore, waiting for him. Besides, I wasn't just itching to tackle that woodpile again.

I hauled myself out of the small, uncomfortable bunk, not sorry I wasn't spending another night in that thing. I stretched, dressed, and walked toward the ranch house. Zeb, who had warmed up to me some after he saw how much wood I'd chopped, stepped out the back door and handed me some coffee. He waved me inside, sat me down at the table and put a mess of bacon in front of me. I had no problem finishing it off. I'd earned it at that woodpile.

When I finished, I pushed back and told Zeb I'd be heading out. I asked him one more time if he had any idea where the guy I'd been looking for might have gone. He started to shake his head no, then stopped. I watched him and waited.

"Well," he said finally. "You could mebbe check down there at Salado. Guy down there has some pretty good harrses," he said grudgingly. "Not as good as mine," he mumbled. "Name's Peterson, has a ranch down there at Salado. You can ask fer him at the Stagecoach Inn."

I rose, tossed the last handful of bacon in my mouth, and trotted out the back door. I knew that Salado was a stop on the Chisholm Trail, and I had heard of the Stagecoach Inn. It was something I could check on. I thanked him over my shoulder, saddled up the gelding, and headed down the trail.

When I reached Salado, I crossed a new bridge over Salado Creek and I found myself looking at an impressive restaurant and hotel with white columns and white railings on the second floor. I dismounted in front and stopped to look at it. I'd been told that Sam Houston, Robert E. Lee and Jesse James had all eaten in the restaurant. I looked down at my dirty clothes and muddy boots and decided I wasn't ready for it this time. Maybe next time I could clean up a little.

A clatter of wheels behind me got my attention, then a small cloud of dust rolled over me. I dusted myself off as best I could, then turned around to see a stage rolling to a stop in front of the inn. A hefty, sour looking driver climbed down off the stage and opened the door for the passengers. I figured the stage driver might be a good source of information about the Peterson ranch and horses. I waited until all the passengers had emptied out of the stage and moved to the inn before I went to question the driver.

I walked over to the stage. The driver's irritated expression faded only slightly when he saw the badge on my chest. He waited impatiently for me to reach him, then folded his arms across his chest.

"Yeah?"

I was just a mite put off by that greeting, I must say. I folded my arms and stared him down until he shifted his feet and broke the stare. "I'm looking for a little information," I said. "In particular, I'd like to know about the Peterson ranch. Where is it, and what kind of horses do they have out there?"

He refused to look at me, staring across the road and shuffling his feet some more. He pointed toward the south. "Down the road, mebbe two miles, you kin see it from the road on the left. They got some harrses, but nuthin' I could use to pull this stage. Harrses that fancy folks might like to prance around on in a parade or somethin'. That's all I know." He turned abruptly and began to unhitch the horses from the wagon.

I started to ask if the stagecoach line had a prize for rude drivers, 'cause he must win every time, but I changed my mind. He'd told me what I needed to know, even if I didn't like the way he said it. I just got on the gelding and headed south.

The Peterson ranch showed up right where he said it would be. A sign hung from the gate after I'd ridden about two miles. A man was working right at the front of the property near the gate when I rode in. He was fixing the fence, and he stopped, put his hands on his hips, and waited as I rode over.

"Mr. Peterson," I asked.

He nodded, took in the badge on my chest, put down his tools and walked over. "Gus," he said, extending a hand. "What kin I do fer ya?"

I shook his hand, then pulled Jessie's drawing out of my pocket. I opened it and started to hand it over to him. "Have you seen…" I started to ask. He drew in his breath sharply and turned to his left, staring toward the barn I could see in the background.

"Wes," he said. "Leastaways, that's what he told me his name was. What's he done?"

I folded the paper back up and put it away, staring over toward the barn. "Well," I said, "I don't know if he's done anything yet, but he seems to keep showing up, looking for work, just a week or two before a ranch gets their horses stolen. Do you raise some high-dollar horses around here, show horses or race horses or some such?"

He was still staring back toward the barn, growing redder in the face by the minute. He tore his gaze away and looked back at me. "Yep," he growled, still glaring in the direction of the barn every couple of seconds. "Moved out here from Virginny, uh, Virginia, a couple o' years ago. Mostly I run cattle now, but I brought some top-notch breeding stock, an' I have some customers back east for my horses. I ship a couple back there every year."

I turned and mounted up. "He's in the barn, right? You keep looking over in that direction." Peterson bobbed his head up and down a couple times.

"Mind if I go talk to him?" I asked.

Peterson waved at the barn. "Go ahead. I'm right behind ya."

As I approached the barn, I could see somebody saddling a horse over there, glancing over his shoulder from time to time. He looked to be in a hurry. As I got closer, he seemed to be trying to decide whether to jump on that horse and light out of there, or stay and talk. He stayed, probably because I was only about ten yards away from him when he finished saddling.

I dismounted and strolled in his direction. "Your name Wes?" I asked.

He hesitated, like he was trying to remember what it was he was calling himself today.

Finally, his head kinda bounced up and down, once or twice. "Yeah," he said. He took a long look at the badge, then turned and seemed to fiddle with his saddle.

I took a few steps closer. "How long you been workin' here, Wes?" He mumbled something I couldn't quite understand, so I took a couple more steps in his direction. "What did you say?"

He wheeled around suddenly with a riding crop in his hand and took a vicious swing at me. I barely ducked out of the way. He turned and jumped on his horse and spurred it away, heading for the gate and the road beyond.

I turned, ran back to the gelding and jumped aboard. We took off, down to the gate, then turned south to follow him down the road. After only several hundred yards, I could see it was no contest. That gelding could really move. We were catching up in a hurry. I could see Wes look behind, that riding crop still in his hand, and it didn't take no genius to see he wanted to use it on me.

I looked down and lifted my lariat off the saddle. I had carried one ever since my days on the cattle drive. I'd done a lot of practicing back then, and I kind of prided myself on it. As the gelding pounded closer, I shook out a loop and dropped it neatly over his shoulders, then pulled it tight. He had no choice but to slow his horse, but there at the end, he didn't slow it enough. He got pulled backwards. He finally yanked his feet out of the stirrups, bounced off the horse's rump, then bounced on his own rump in the middle of the road.

He got up, but that gelding had gotten some fine training, I could see that right away. He backed right up, dumped the man back on the road, and kept that line taught. Every time that guy started to get some slack in the line, that gelding backed up again. I decided to let Wes roost there in the road for a while. I also decided I had to ask about buying that gelding. He was gettin' more work done today than I was.

After a while I got down, took a short length of rope and tied his hands behind his back. Then I tied his feet together, took off the lariat I'd lassoed him with and put it back on the gelding. I walked over and squatted down beside him in the dirt. "Let's talk about horse stealing," I said.

He swore and spit into the dirt. "I ain't talkin' to you about nuthin'," he informed me.

"OK," I said, "I'll just tie you into that saddle of yours and take you to the nearest sheriff around here. Maybe somebody's heard of you or knows something about you."

He swore some more for a while, then said: "I ain't getting' back in that saddle. Ain't nuthin' you can do about it."

I picked him up, walked over to his horse, and chunked him face down across the saddle. I heard the air whoosh out of him when his belly hit the leather. I picked up the reins and started to walk him back to the gelding.

I heard a muffled voice from the other side of the horse. "OK," he said. "I'll sit up and you can tie me in."

"Now ain't that nice," I said. "I love it when folks can agree on things."

I got my rope back out and tied his horse to my saddle. We walked back to the Peterson ranch, where I was told that the nearest sheriff was back in Belton. I was headed back that way, anyway. Peterson looked like he wanted to use my rope for a noose, but I just took my prisoner out of there, headed north to Belton.

Holt wasted no time getting away from the meeting spot where he had left Lance. He didn't want to take any chances on that posse coming back. He walked his horse back out to the river and stayed in the shallow water for several hundred yards before weaving through the trees and finally taking the trail back to Granger. If Lance found any tracks, he wouldn't make a connection. And chances were, heading back to Granger was the last thing Lance would think about doing, anyway.

A day and a half of hard riding brought Holt back to the Longhorn Canyon. He found Ike and Slade napping under a tree when he rode up in the early afternoon. One of them woke when he rode up to them, then nudged the other awake. They both stared at him wordlessly.

Holt jerked a thumb at Ike. "We're riding in ten minutes. We'll be gone maybe three, four days. Pack up and saddle up." He rode away, not seeing the hateful glares that followed him. He wouldn't have cared if he had seen them, anyway.

Another two days' ride saw them pass through Belton and on down the road to the Maitlin ranch. They rode past, Holt noticing as he did that there was a dog who barked at them as they rode by. He would have to remember the dog and do something about that.

They circled the ranch and came in from the west side as the sun was setting. Holt took out his binoculars and found a vantage point to look things over. The horses he saw were mustangs— cowboy horses, not what he was looking for.

Still keeping a respectful distance, he worked closer to the house. He spotted a small corral at the back of the house and refocused the binoculars. A small smile appeared on his face. These were worth stealing. He swept the lens back and forth, then stopped on the stallion. He looked up, then back down through the glass. A small whistle escaped his lips. This one, he thought, was worth keeping for himself. He lowered the binoculars, looked around in all directions, then moved in a little closer.

Chapter Seven
Footprints

Jessie sat on the back porch of the house, keeping one eye on the horses in the corral. She and Kyle had both worked closer to the house and corral these last two days, reluctant to leave her prize horses unguarded. Keeping them safe at night was a different matter entirely; she'd had very little sleep last night. The drowsiness from the late afternoon sun today was almost overpowering.

She found it very unsettling that the man who'd asked for work the other day may have been trying to size up the herd. Her instincts had been right: At least she had sent him away before he could have gotten a good look at her stallion and prize mares. That thought comforted her a little, but only a little. He could have simply asked around town in Belton to find out more about her herd.

She wondered if Ash had been able to find the man. She was also wondering when he might be back. It had been a great comfort to have him here. And, she had to admit to herself; it wasn't entirely about guarding the horses. A small smile spread across her face, and the drowsiness took over. She leaned back in her rocking chair and dozed off.

She came awake when her dog, who had been sleeping in the sunshine on the porch, growled. Jessie came awake and looked at the dog who was looking off to the west, past the corral, alternating growls with an occasional bark. Jessie came to her feet, still watching her dog. "What is it, Rex?"

The dog came to his feet and trotted down the steps, still growling, his attention fixed on the trees west of the pasture. He disappeared into the trees. Jessie grabbed the Henry rifle she had propped up in the corner of the porch and followed the path taken by her dog. A moment later, the dog burst into frenzied barking. Jessie held the rifle out in front of her and broke into a crouching run, trying to follow the sound of the barking.

The trees slowed her progress as she entered the woods. She stopped from time to time and listened, but the barking was growing fainter. She reached the edge of the tree line on the far side of the woods, but saw nothing in the pasture that opened up before her. She cast back and forth along the tree line and saw a few faint horse tracks leading out into the pasture. She could follow them for only about twenty yards before she lost the trail. She didn't want to leave the horses unguarded, so she didn't pursue it any farther.

She returned to the trees and followed the horse tracks back into the woods. The earth was a little more moist here than in the meadow. She made some progress following the tracks until she found the place where the horse had been tethered. There were many tracks here, circling back and forth around an oak tree with a large, low-hanging limb. She began to look for human footprints leading away from the tree, but found she couldn't make much progress. The man was obviously lighter than the horse, so the impressions left were much more shallow.

Jessie could identify only three faints prints leading away from the oak tree. She was pretty sure she could see partial prints from a boot heel for a few yards, but then she found nothing more. She blew out a breath of frustration, then a sound behind her caused her to wheel around, rifle at the ready. She felt relief wash over her when she saw it was her dog, Rex, returning. She called the dog and let him sniff around the oak tree, wondering if he could give her some direction.

Rex sniffed the ground around the oak tree, then trotted away toward the ranch house, pausing once in a while to sniff the ground and the bushes. Jessie followed slowly, stopping often to check the woods behind her, afraid there was a second man out there. Or, she thought, this first man could have turned around and come back.

She heard the dog snuffling eagerly near another large oak tree in front of her. She pushed through the branches blocking her way and scanned the ground where the dog had stopped. She caught her breath when she spotted a clear boot print on the ground near the tree. The point of the boot mark was aimed toward the ranch.

She lifted her eyes and saw that the man, whoever he was, had seen the horse corral pretty clearly from here.

Jessie stood indecisively for a moment, then untied the ribbon she'd used to tie back her hair this morning. She wrapped around a tree limb to help her mark the spot, then started toward the house. Something stopped her, and she turned around and went back to look at the boot print. She stepped a few feet to the side and pressed her own boot into the ground, then stood back to compare the prints. They were pretty much the same size. Puzzled, she took another look. Her brother, Kyle would leave a much bigger print. Her mother, Iris, had a boot size a bit smaller than her own. She was sure the first print was not hers.

She turned and trotted through the trees toward the house. When she came out of the woods, she could see Kyle pitching hay just beyond the other side of the corral. She cupped her hands and shouted his name, then waved toward the house when he looked up. She ran up the back steps, left the Henry in the corner of the kitchen, then pulled a piece of paper and pencil out of the cupboard.

She was finishing the note as the back door slammed and Kyle moved over to look at the note. She re-read what she had just written:

Ash,

Someone has been watching the house. I found

a boot print in the woods, not too far from the

corral. It's a small print, so I'm not sure if it was a man or a woman. Please come as soon as

you can.

Jessie

She let Kyle finish reading the note, then folded it up and gave it to him. "You've got to find Ash," she said. "Ride back to Belton first and ask for him there—maybe the sheriff's office and the saloon, anyplace else you can think of."

Kyle nodded, grabbed the note, and ran out through the back door. In just a few minutes he had saddled a horse, and Jessie heard the hoof beats dying off in the distance as he galloped away.

The sheriff stepped outside of his office in Belton as I rode up, leading Wes, or whatever his name was, behind me. The sheriff hooked his thumbs inside his belt as I untied Wes from the saddle, then untied his feet and pulled him off the saddle. Then I stood him up and pushed him toward the jail. The sheriff held the door and followed me into the office/county jail. He watched as I pulled out a chair and told my prisoner to sit down.

"Elmer Hutchins," he said to me, extending his hand. He waggled a toothpick between his lips. "Whattcha got here?"

I shook the sheriff's hand, then pointed at Wes, scowling from where he sat in the chair. I turned to look at Elmer, pulling Jessie's drawing from my pocket. I explained how Wes seemed to show up at ranches and ask for work just a few days before they stole valuable horses. His eyebrows lifted as he compared the drawing to Wes, sitting in front of him.

"Where'd the drawing come from?" he asked.

I told him that Jessie Maitlin had drawn it when Wes had applied for work at the Maitlin ranch. The name worked like I'd hoped it would; his expression changed to a frown when he looked back at Wes. He pulled a chair out, turned it around and straddled it backwards, his arms folded over the top of the chair back.

"I don't take kindly to folks coming to my county to rob people," he began. "What do you have to say for yourself?"

Wes' gaze went to the floor and stayed there. He shrugged and said nothing as Hutchins continued to fire questions at him.

"Who're you workin' for? What were you doing out at the Maitlin place? Where are you from?"

After several minutes of silence, Hutchins looked up at me, shrugged and looked back at Wes. "Well," he said, "we can just lock you up in the jail an' see if you're less bashful in a few days." When he still got no answer, he stood up and pushed the chair away. "We'll give you a couple meals a day in here. Of course, the new cook down to the café just got hisself promoted from washin' dishes a couple days ago. We gen'rally let the new cooks practice on the prisoners for a few days before reg'lar folks eat the food."

Still getting no answers, he hauled Wes to his feet and pulled him back to the cells at the back. He pushed Wes through the door, locked it, then told him to turn around. He cut the rope around Wes' hands through the bars.

I stood in the hallway, then noticed the glare Wes sent my direction. Pure hatred. I guess he didn't cotton much to getting yanked off that horse onto his caboose, back there in the road. I stared back at him, then took a couple steps forward. "If you show up at the Maitlin place again," I told him, "your tail end ain't the only thing that's gonna be ailing you."

Hutchins moved back out to the door, motioning at me to come out on the porch with him. "I can keep him here for a few days and send a description to some other sheriffs and marshals around here—see if anybody matches that description or if he matches any posters they have. If nobody claims him, I'll have to let him go after a few days."

I nodded. The prisoner hadn't actually done anything wrong that we could prove. I could just hope he was already wanted by somebody already. If not, I hoped he would decide this wasn't worth it and move on.

I moved down the steps and mounted my horse. "Can you let me know if you have to let him go?" I asked. "I'll be out at the Maitlin place for a few days." Hutchins nodded and waved, and I moved across the street and down a few doors to the telegraph office. I dashed off a note, telling Captain McDonald about Wes, and that the sheriff in Belton had him in jail right now. I told him I had a drawing I would send in if he wanted it. Then I mounted up and headed for Jessie's ranch.

As I reached the edge of town, I could see somebody coming from the other way, riding at a full-out gallop. I pulled over a bit and eased up on my reins, not wanting to sideswipe whoever this was coming at me. As the rider drew closer, I recognized him. It was Jessie's brother, Kyle.

Just as he was about to go past me, he saw me and began slowing the horse. He actually overran me by several yards before he could get his horse stopped and turned. I sat and waited, half-turned in his direction. He began to talk as he came alongside, the words just spilling out of him. I couldn't tell who was more out of breath, Kyle or his horse.

"Mr. McKinnon," he sputtered, "Jessie sent me. Somebody's been there, at the ranch, spyin' on things, lookin' it over."

That got my attention. "How do you know? Did you see somebody?"

"Footprints," he said. "Jessie saw footprints. He..." Kyle seemed to remember something and began fishing around in his pockets. He held a note out to me. "Here," he said. "Jessie said to give you this."

I grabbed the note and began to read. My eyes got big when I saw the part about the small boot print, and I shoved the note into my pocket. "Let's go!" I shouted. We galloped out of town, heading north for the ranch.

Mike Stone waved goodbye to his wife Sarah and turned his horse on to the trail toward Austin. His visit at home had been all too short. It was the one thing he didn't like about working for the Rangers. He was away from home too much. He supposed that he might be able to stay closer to home if he worked his way up to captain. He pulled his watch from his pocket and checked it. He had a nine o'clock meeting with Captain McDonald, and he needed to pick up the pace if he didn't want to be late. About twenty minutes later, he knocked on the captain's door.

McDonald waved him in immediately, pointing at a chair across the desk from him. "Good to see you, Stone," he said. "Everything good at home?" Stone nodded, surprised at any personal greeting from the boss. "I sent you a telegram about Red Corbin, right?" McDonald asked, changing the tone and subject immediately.

Stone nodded again and stared silently at the floor. Red's death wasn't something he wanted to talk about just yet. McDonald sensed the mood change and waited a few moments before continuing.

"I've got Ash McKinnon out near Belton right now, following up on a letter from a rancher out there, somebody who thinks they might be scouting her place out, with a robbery in mind. I want you to go out there and join McKinnon for a few days, see what's he's got." McDonald paused, suddenly remembering his last telegram from Stone.

"What did you find up there, up north? You said you wanted to look into something that maybe had to do with the horse stealing."

Stone nodded and explained about the small horse racing track built just off the Chisholm Trail in North Texas. The horse he'd seen might not have been one one they were looking for, he said, but it looked like somebody had worked the brand over with a running iron. The guy riding that horse, he added, had left in a hurry when he saw a badge.

McDonald digested that information, leaning back in his chair and clasping his hands behind his head. "So," he said, "you think maybe they steal the horses and run them in races." Stone nodded. "Up north of here, along the Chisholm Trail?" he continued.

Stone shrugged, then nodded. "Some of them could be up there, being raced in The Nation, Kansas, along the Chisholm Trail. Maybe some of them are good enough they ship 'em back east for breeding and racing. Maybe out to California too, for some racing or breeding." He lapsed into thoughtful silence for a moment. "Somebody would have to be pretty well organized. Stealing just the ones they want and shipping them out with nobody figuring out where they've gone. Somebody selling them, wherever that is they go."

McDonald turned his chair around and studied a map on the wall behind him. Stone could see several small circles drawn in red in a semicircle north and east of Austin. "That's where they've been stolen," he said over his shoulder. Stone got up and moved around the desk to get a closer look at the map. He could see circles in Lampasas, Belton, Salado, and another down to the south near San Antonio.

"I wonder where they're going?" McDonald said, half to himself. We've been on the lookout for them all around Central Texas, some in East Texas, North Texas. That one you saw at the race up there, if it was one of them, is the first one we've run across." He turned back around and pulled two written sheets of paper from the desk.

"That's the descriptions of the horses taken," he said. "See if maybe the one you saw matched up with anything on that list."

Stone ran his finger down the first page, then turned the page over and started on the second one. Halfway down the page, his finger stopped. "This one could be it," he said. "Black gelding, rocking R brand, about fifteen and a half hands. That one had a circle R brand, but that could be done with a running iron, easy enough."

"That's probably one of 'em then," McDonald said thoughtfully, still staring at the map. "Where do they go? Railroad?"

Stone walked around the desk again. "The Missouri-Kansas-Texas Railroad runs right down through here," he said, tracing a line from Kansas, down through the Indian Territory and through the

Dallas-Ft. Worth area to Austin. "I guess they could put the horses on the railroad somewhere down here and ship them out." He stopped and gazed at the map. "I don't know how they would get them to the railroad with nobody seeing them, or how they would get the stolen horses on the train."

"Mmmph," McDonald said, turning back around. "Don't know how they get them sold, either, when they get where they're going. Who could get all that set up and keep it running?"

Stone shook his head and walked back around to stand beside his chair. He sensed this was just about over. McDonald never went in for any chit-chat.

McDonald stared absently at his desk for a minute, then raised his head, picked up a pen, and pulled over a stack of papers. "OK, keep thinking about it," he said. "Go see what McKinnon's got going out there. Maitlin ranch, a little north of Belton." He picked up the paper on the top of the stack, muttering to himself.

Stone half smiled and nodded, knowing he'd been dismissed. "Cap'n," he said, half under his breath. He put on his hat and let himself out.

Chapter Eight
Robbed

When we were about a mile away from the ranch, I slowed my horse to a stop. Kyle pulled up alongside me. "If there's anybody watching the ranch now, which I'm guessing there are some folks doing just that," I began, "I don't want them to know that I'm here." I pointed down the road. "I'm going to ride past the house and come back in through the trees on the west side. That's where you said the boot prints are, right?"

Kyle nodded. "Yes, sir. In the trees, on a line with that corral where we put the horses. Maybe seventy-five or a hundred yards away."

"Good," I said. "That's where I'm headed. I'll take the last part of it on foot once I'm into the trees. You can tell Jessie to meet me over there and show me the tracks."

Kyle wasted no time, clucking to his horse and trotting on down the road. I waited several minutes, then followed, but moved on past the entrance to the house and pulled over into the woods to the west. I dismounted and wove in through the trees. When I reached a place even with the corral on my right, I tethered my horse and waited.

I heard footsteps coming after about ten minutes and watched carefully through the trees to be sure it was Jessie coming before I revealed myself. After I saw both Jessie and Kyle coming toward me, I stepped out from behind a tree and called to them. They altered course slightly and walked over. Jessie stopped beside a large oak about twenty yards away and motioned for me to come over.

I walked to her, and she pointed to the ground. There was a clear boot print, tiny for a man's print. I pulled Red's drawing from my pocket, squatted down, and compared the two. The print on the ground was exactly the size of the one in the drawing.

Jessie knelt beside me and stared at the drawing. "Where's that from?" she asked. I handed her the drawing and let her compare it to the print on the ground.

"That was drawn by my friend Red, just before he died," I said sadly. "He was the Ranger working the case before me. He was bushwhacked, shot from ambush, over west of here after a robbery near Lampasas."

She folded the drawing back up and handed it to me. "And this was in his pocket?"

I shook my head. "No, whoever shot him must have taken everything in his pockets. He left this with some clothes, at the last place he stayed. Friends of mine, Mike and Sarah Stone. I'm hoping they will send Mike to join me on this case," I added as an afterthought.

I stood and continued to look at the boot print. Jessie stood and waited for me to say what I was thinking. "I want to stay out here until nighttime, then I'll be watching for them to come back. Tonight seems likely. Not much moon out these next few days. That'll help them." I looked around. "I'll move back from here a little, where there's good cover. Good chance he'll come back to get another look from this spot before he moves in."

Jessie moved a little closer. "Do you have a bedroll with you?" I nodded. "Anything else you might need? A couple blankets? It's been cold at night," she reminded me.

I said yes to the blankets. She turned around to Kyle. "Can you run in and get a couple blankets for Ash?"

Kyle trotted off to get the blankets, and Jessie turned back around. "Are you hungry? I can bring you some food in a bit."

I said yes to the food as well. There was a little smile on her face. "I didn't think you would turn down the food," she said.

Was it my imagination, or was she standing a little closer to me than she needed to? I hoped she was, but I doubted myself a bit on that one. I mean, what with bringing in the prisoner and hustling to get over here, I hadn't even had a shave in about three days. I figured my face must be getting a mite bristly.

I glanced at her and passed a hand over my face without thinking about it. Her laugh was a very pleasant sound. She patted my shoulder.

"Don't worry, you're a very welcome sight to me. I'm glad you're here." She turned to go. "And not just because I'm worried about the horses." She turned and walked back to the house. The door closed softly behind her.

Well, I thought to myself, if that don't beat all. I moved back farther into the trees, searching for a spot to pitch my bedroll and keep an eye out for whoever made that small boot print.

Holt squatted in front of a small fire, warming his hands against the January chill in the night air. They had retreated more than a mile away from the Maitlin ranch, he estimated. Tonight was the night he wanted to make his move. He glanced over at Ike, who was whistling tunelessly while he whittled away on a stick. Holt rolled his eyes in irritation, then stood up and walked away from the flames. He never looked directly into the fire—he didn't want to be blinded if anyone walked up on the camp. Still, he needed a minute to let his vision adjust.

A small plan was forming in his mind. It was a little risky, but he wasn't a patient man, and the risk seemed worth it just to get things moving. He wanted more money, and he wanted it quickly. To do that, he needed to get some information. Maybe he could use the horses they would steal tonight to help him do that.

Maybe he could shortcut the handoff to Lance and the connection in Temple. Lance was probably still licking his wounds after getting his bank robbery money stolen. Maybe he would even be a little slow to get in touch with The Boss, whoever that was, after Holt didn't show up with the horses.

Meanwhile, he would have to break in to the railroad agent's house in Temple to find out, if he could, who these horses were going to. What was the name of that town? Oh yes, it was Parsons, Kansas. If he could get a name to work with up there, maybe he could take these horses, hide them out while he broke in to the agent's house in Temple, then get on the train with the horses. He would have to do that farther north, maybe Waco. And maybe he could make a deal for himself with whoever it was in Kansas to buy the horses from him. It was risky, but it could be a pretty sweet setup.

Satisfied with his idea, Holt turned and saw Ike asleep on the ground. The knife and whittled stick were laying beside him, and he was snoring. Holt walked over and kicked him, none too gently, on the leg. "Let's move," he snapped.

They saddled quickly and began riding toward the ranch. Holt went over his plan for the second time, wanting no misunderstandings or mistakes. "I'm coming in from the west. I'm going to look things over first from the woods over there. You will circle around to the north and get close to the corral, but not close enough to disturb the horses. You wait for me. When I come over and give the signal, you ride over and open the corral. I'm going to rope the stallion. You pick one or two mares, rope them, and we get out of there fast." Holt looked over, but couldn't see Ike's face in the dark.

"Got it?" Holt snarled. He hadn't heard an answer and felt his temper rising.

"Sure, sure," came the answer. "I wait until I hear from you, I open the gate, we steal the horses." They rode the rest of the way in silence.

They parted near the ranch. Holt rode to the woods, going in on horseback only a few yards before dismounting and moving forward on foot. He found it much harder to find his way in the dark. He cursed softly to himself as he cast back and forth, trying to find his way back to his vantage point. He couldn't count on Ike to do as told if it took too much longer, he knew. After about ten minutes of searching, he finally spotted the tree he'd stood beside when he had been here earlier. He moved over to it.

He unslung his binoculars and checked the house. Everything seemed quiet. Satisfied, he turned to check Ike's position before moving out to give Ike the OK. Then he would move to the corral. His mouth dropped open, and he stifled another curse. Ike was at the corral gate, reaching down to open it. Holt stood stock still for a moment, trying to decide what to do. Then he heard a stick snap behind him. His hand dropped to his gun, and he drew as he turned.

It was a cloudy night with just a sliver of a moon showing. It couldn't have been a better night for horse rustling, unfortunately. I had grown up in the woods, and I was counting on those skills to help me tonight. They had the advantage—they knew what the plan was. All we could do was wait for them and hope to stop 'em. I glanced over toward the porch, knowing that Jessie was sitting up there with her Henry rifle. She would fire only toward the corral, if she fired at all. I would fire only away from the house. She wouldn't come into my field of fire and I wouldn't go into hers.

As the hours wore on, the coffee Jessie had brought me for dinner had long since worn off. I couldn't walk around keeping myself awake, for fear of making noise. I swung my arms back and forth, both to stay awake and to keep warm. From time to time I stopped and picked up the blankets and wrapped them around me.

Mostly I kept focused on that spot where somebody had left prints. I moved my eyes back and forth, not locking in, hoping to pick up movement from the corner of my eyes. Finally, I heard rustling noises. They were very faint at first, then I was sure they were coming in my direction. Finally, someone in black clothes passed by, moving slowly and only briefly illuminated by the faint glimmer of moonlight breaking through the cover of the trees overhead. I held still and watched as he took up a position under the oak tree.

He appeared to be half-turned toward me, but he seemed to be focused completely on the house. Then he turned a little more toward the corral. I eased out of the thicket where I'd been standing and started cat-footin' it in his direction. I had to crawl, but I knew if I didn't keep coming, he was bound to start toward the corral soon. I picked up the pace a little, testing each step before putting my weight down on my foot. It was so dark out here; I knew I needed a little luck.

When I was still a few steps away, he shifted and seemed to mutter something under his breath. I figured one more cat-step and then I'd rush... my foot came down on a stick and there was a loud snap. I came the rest of the way with a rush, my hand dropping to my pistol, but as he turned, I could see that his gun was already out. I swung a haymaker left hook and connected with a solid crunching noise to the right side of his jaw. He spun and fell backwards, but I heard the roar of his gun just as I felt a crashing blow to my head. Then I blacked out.

Jessie was sitting on the back porch with her Henry rifle cradled across her lap. She was bundled up against the January cold, and it seemed like several hours had passed. She regretted that she hadn't taken Kyle up on his offer to take her place and watch for the second half of the night.

She shifted, then sat up straight, staring out past the corral. Someone was approaching slowly on horseback. She leaned forward and balanced the Henry on the railing, sighting down the barrel. The man seemed indecisive, sitting on his horse just beyond the gate at the far side of the corral. Then he reached down to open the gate. She aimed the rifle at his shoulder and slowly squeezed as the gate swung open.

Suddenly there was a gunshot from the trees. Startled, she pulled the rifle just slightly and missed her target when she fired. The horses, startled by the shots, bolted from the corral. She swung the Henry back to the man on the horse and fired again. He was moving now, but she saw him arch his back suddenly. She was pretty sure she had grazed him Then he grabbed his rope, shook out a loop, and dropped it over the neck of one of her mares as the horse galloped past. The man disappeared in the darkness before she could get off another shot.

Leaping down from the porch, she whirled as Kyle bolted out through the back door. "Get the horses!" she shouted, then turned toward the woods where Ash had taken up watch for the night. She ran toward the trees, then stopped, then began trotting quietly toward Ash's position again. She didn't dare call out his name. There was no telling who had fired that shot.

She reached the tree line south of where she had been that afternoon, working her way silently forward. After a few minutes, there was a thrashing noise off to her right. She lifted the Henry, then held her fire. More thrashing noises followed, then she faintly heard a horse galloping away. Feeling more confident that only Ash was out here now, she began calling his name softly. She heard no answer.

Jessie felt a little disoriented in trying to find the spot where Ash had set up camp in the near-total darkness. She decided to come back out of the trees and enter the way she had before—farther north. Coming from that entry point, she felt sure she could find it.

Bending down and holding low, just in case Ash heard noises and fired toward the corral. That was assuming he was in any shape to fire. She found her entry point and came back into the woods, moving west and looking for the large oak tree where she had seen the boot print. As she worked in closer, a low moan guided her for the last twenty yards. Now she could see someone lying on the ground and moving one arm back and forth in the leaves. She risked striking a match and saw that it was Ash, lying on his back with a nasty, bloody furrow across the side of his head.

Jessie knelt down beside him, touching his arm and saying his name softly, but he didn't respond, and his eyes remained closed.

She looked around, then struck another match and found her way to his camp. Jessie looked through his saddlebag and found his canteen, then picked up the lantern she had brought out earlier this evening. She bent down and picked up one of the old blankets she had brought him, then returned to where Ash was, tearing a small piece off the blanket as she walked.

She again knelt and looked around. Feeling sure the attackers had left when the horses stampeded, she struck another match and lit the lantern. She turned his head gently to examine the head wound, then poured some water from the canteen onto the torn-out piece of the blanket. She washed his face and forehead gently. After about a minute or two, he stirred and his eyes opened.

He started to rise, then moaned and fell back on the blanket. "Easy, Ash," she whispered. "It's me. I think they have gone. Just lay there for a minute." He nodded his head slowly, even that small motion causing more pain, judging by the look on his face. After another minute or two, she resumed washing his face and hands with the moistened piece of blanket.

He stopped moaning after a bit, and Jesse stopped. His eyes were still open, and he seemed to track her movements when she changed positions. She took his wrist and felt the pulse. It was strong and steady.

She whirled when she heard a rustling noise behind her. She felt for the Henry with one hand, rising and turning. She sighed in relief when she saw the light of another lantern. Iris came through the trees and knelt beside them. "Is he OK?" she asked.

"I think so." Jesse turned and looked at Ash. "I think I need to pour a little water on that wound to clean it out," she said. "Do you think you can let me do that?"

Ash looked a bit puzzled, then raised a hand toward his head. He felt gently of his scalp, wincing when his fingers touched the furrow where the bullet had passed. He winced and put his hand back down. Reaching with his other hand, he grasped Jessie's free hand. "Go ahead," he breathed.

Jessie opened the canteen again and poured a little water on the wound, letting the bits of leaves and dirt wash away. Ash made no sound as she poured. When she had cleaned it as best she could, she stopped and put the canteen away. She looked at Iris. "I'm afraid to move him right now," she said. "Can you stay with him and keep him as comfortable as you can? I'm going for the doctor."

"Yes," Iris whispered. Jessie turned back to Ash and squeezed his hand, a little surprised to realize she was still holding it. "I'm going for the doctor, Ash" she said. She reached out to pick up his pistol, lying on the ground just a foot or two away. She placed it beside him. "Here's your gun," she said. "Mom will be here, and she'll have my Henry. I'm riding into town for the doctor." She leaned down and gave him a kiss on the cheek. "I'll be right back."

Chapter Nine
Recovery and Revenge

I was only partly aware of the people crowding around me. I knew Iris had been talking to me, and I knew that Jessie came back with an older guy I hadn't seen before. He set a black bag down next to me, and I figured out he was the town doctor. I stared up at him. But it was hard to see, as some sunlight was filtering through the trees. I squinted at him, feeling a little dizzy and clenching my teeth against the headache.

"How you feeling?" he asked. "I'm Doc Linden." He grabbed my jaw and turned my head to the side.

"I been better," I said, letting out a grunt when he turned my head. "Except I feel a little addle-headed."

"Mmmph," he said, fixing me with a stare. "More addle-headed than usual, I guess." He stared into my eyes for a while. "I expect you've got a rock-hard head and you're gonna be fine." He turned my head again. "How many do you see?"

I rolled my eyes at Jessie and stared at him. "I only see one of you doc, and I'm thinkin' maybe it's one more than I wanna see."

He snorted again and waved his hand in the air. "Fingers, man. How many fingers do you see?"

"Oh." I looked at his hand. "Two. I see two."

He put his head down to my chest and listened for a while. "Sounds OK," he said. He sat back and looked me over. "Anything else you got complaints about?"

I lifted my left hand in the air. "I don't think it's broke," I said, "but maybe you can look it over." He took my hand and looked at it. It was bruised up and swollen some. "What did you run into with this?" he asked.

I grinned for the first time in a while. "I ran that into a horse rustler's jaw," I said with satisfaction. "Punched him good, right in the jaw. Right before he shot me in the head, I mean."

Doc Linden chuckled a little and looked at my hand. He told me to wiggle my fingers and wave my hand up and down. Everything seemed to work.

"Yeah, he's OK," he announced. "Help me get him up." He stooped down to give me a hand, but I wasn't a whole lot of help. He waved at Jessie and Iris to give him a hand. Between the three of them, they got me up, and we took a slow walk to the house.

We reached the front room, and the doc looked at Jessie. "Where do you want this big lug? He weighs a ton," he added.

Jessie steered us toward her bedroom. "On my bed," she said.

The doc's eyebrows went up, and I guess mine did too. "You don't wanna put me in there," I said. "I might break that bed or something." I started to point at the couch in the front room.

Jessie laid two fingers across my lips. "Ash," she said, "this is my house, and you got hurt stopping horse rustlers from stealing my stock. You just go where I say. You'll get the best sleep in the bed. I'll sleep on the couch."

The doctor chortled at that one. "I guess she told you," he said. They laid me on the bed, and I gotta admit, it felt pretty good. Until the doc started washing off the wound, that is. I clenched my teeth again and tried not to whimper out loud. After that, he wrapped a big bandage around my head; kinda made me look like one of those mummies in Egypt. Finally, he finished. He waggled a finger at me. "Three days of rest," he said. "No running around punching people on the jaw. Unless, of course, they're trying to shoot your fool head off again."

Jessie saw him out the front door and came back to stand by the bed. "I think I'm his favorite," I told her.

She laughed pretty hard. Then she sat down beside me on the bed. "He's a little grumpy, I know, but he's been a good doctor for us. I actually think he likes you. Besides, who knows, maybe you can be somebody else's favorite."

I wasn't sure what she meant, but I knew what I hoped she meant. I let it go, though, on account of my addle-headed condition. I had to allow for that. I started to talk, but it seemed like my eyelids just kept rolling down on me. I dropped off to sleep before I knew it.

Holt rode west, clinging to the saddle horn with one hand, reins in the same hand. His other hand was holding on to his jaw. It jarred him and ached savagely each time his horse's hooves hit the ground. He had the vague impression he had shot a man with a badge on his chest as he went down. He remembered the roar of his gun, but he had blacked out immediately afterwards.

When he had come to, he had heard a woman's voice calling someone's name. He assumed it was the name of the man he had shot. He gathered himself together, stumbled to his horse, and got out of there. He had a pre-arranged meeting place with Ike, and he just hoped to get there before he passed out again.

When he came close to passing out, Holt reined in the horse, dismounted, and put his head between his knees. He wondered if he had killed the man he'd shot. If not, he wanted to find him someday and finish the job. He touched his jaw gingerly and wondered if it was broken. Finally, he remounted and pushed on.

As the sun came up behind him, Holt recognized both their meeting place and the figure of Ike, who was dismounted in a small circle of trees. He was squatting in front of a small fire, warming his hands. When he turned slightly, Holt could see a bloody streak across his back. Ike's jacket and shirt were torn. Holt found a twisted satisfaction in knowing that Ike had been injured too. Until that moment, he had been torn between killing Ike for opening the gate too soon back there, or letting him live because Holt still needed him.

Holt dismounted and walked up to Ike with his hand balled up into a fist. He'd intended to hit Ike, but two things stopped him. One, Ike was bigger, and two, if Ike hit him back on the jaw, the pain would be excruciating. Holt settled for raking him over the coals for about fifteen minutes. Ike accepted the tongue-lashing quietly, but Holt thought he looked absolutely bored.

Finally, Holt's jaw couldn't take any more screaming and he lapsed into silence. He walked over to look at what Ike had brought away from the corral. There was a mare that looked pretty valuable, and a colt that had apparently followed his mother after Ike lassoed her. Somewhat mollified, Holt went back and stood with his back to the fire. The wound across Ike's back was clearly the result of being grazed by a bullet. Holt didn't ask. He splashed water from his canteen onto a rag and bathed his jaw gently.

As the morning wore on, he could see that he was having trouble making himself understood when he talked to Ike. He knew the jaw must still be swelling and probably turning colors by now. He decided he would have to change plans and take a few days here to recover.

Holt turned to Ike, speaking slowly in order to make himself understood. "Go back to Longhorn," he said, irritated that Ike kept looking at his jaw while he talked. "Wait a few days, then go back to that ranch with Slade and steal the stallion. Take it back to Longhorn and wait for me there." He waved a hand in anger when Ike objected. "Do it," he hissed. "Leave these horses with me. Go now."

He watched as Ike shrugged, gathered up his horse's reins and swung aboard. He couldn't choke back a moan of pain as the movement pulled on the bullet wound running across his back. Holt stood, arms folded, and watched him ride away. Then he touched his jaw again, gently. He would stay right here for a couple days, then find a place to hide the horses near Temple while he broke into the station agent's house. Maybe then he could figure a way to take these horses north himself and sell them.

Holt opened his saddlebag and began looking for something he could eat. He cursed softly to himself, wondering how long it would be before he could chew again. Whoever that was wearing the badge back there, Holt promised himself, would pay for this.

Three days later, his jaw feeling a little better, but his mood not improved at all, Holt left his hiding place. The stolen horses were roped and trailing along behind him. He had used a running iron to alter the brands somewhat. He had to admit that he wasn't all that skilled with the iron, but he hoped he had changed the brands enough to cover up the theft. He suspected that his buyers at the other end of this, wherever that was, didn't really care that much about brands.

Holt struck a course to the north and east, angling back toward Temple. He needed to break into the railroad agent's house and find some information and how to sell these horses. What was the name again? He puzzled over that one in his head for a few miles, then remembered: Pendleton. He would take his time getting there. That would give a few more days for his handiwork with the running iron to heal over on the horse's hindquarters, and it would give a little time for any pursuit from the horse rustling to settle down.

He decided his jaw had healed enough to do a little more chewing than he'd been doing, so he pulled the horses off into a stand of post oak trees and picketed them, then settled down with his rifle to wait for the whitetail deer to start moving at sundown. He had seen them everywhere the last couple nights. He didn't have long to wait, dropping a small buck with the first shot. He field-dressed the animal, taking just a few choice cuts, which he grilled over a small fire.

By morning, he was ready to move the horses back east. He didn't want to board the train at Temple, but he needed to move in that direction, north and east, then hide the animals while he went to see what he could find at Pendleton's house. He spent the entire day drifting east. When he came to the railroad tracks for the Missouri-Kansas-Texas railroad, he pulled back into the trees and followed alongside the tracks. By mid-morning the next day, he had built a makeshift corral in a small clearing in a thick stand of post oak and cedar trees. He stood back from the corral to evaluate his work. It wouldn't win any prizes, but he decided it would hold the horses for a couple days and they should be able to graze sufficiently in the area within the corral.

Holt waited until it was nearly sundown before proceeding into Temple. His plan was to wait near the railroad station and, if possible, follow Pendleton home from a distance. If it looked like Pendleton lived alone, he would break into the house or boardinghouse room the next day after Pendleton went to work. If there was a wife at home during the day, he would have to think of something else.

Before leaving for the trip into town, Holt knew he needed to disguise himself as best he could. He had been at the train station, hanging around and asking questions, just a week before. He ran a hand over his beard, then reluctantly poured some water into a pan he used for boiling water and cooking, then pulled the knife from his belt. Twenty minutes later, after several nicks and much cursing, he ran his hand back over his face. It felt strange to his touch, but he knew he would be hard to recognize without his usual heavy beard.

Riding into town, he stopped first at the telegraph office and sent a message to his normal contact, Lance, to tell him that the robbery at the Maitlin ranch had failed. He gave no details, but promised he could rustle the horses within the next week. He sent off the message, confident he had bought himself a little time. He hoped that within a week or two he would have no further need for Lance.

Holt crossed the street and moved down to a saloon. He took a seat near a window, giving him a view of the street. The railroad office was just a few blocks away, and he hoped that Pendleton would come in this direction when he left work. Most of the houses and boarding houses seemed to be on this side of town. Holt remembered Lance talking to a burly man with a thick mustache when he'd brought the horses from the last robbery. He felt pretty safe in assuming that man was Pendleton, and he would be able to recognize him if he came in this direction.

Half an hour later, his hunch proved correct. The man with the luxurious black mustache came down the street toward him. Holt had a moment of panic when he saw that Pendleton was coming into the saloon, but he reminded himself that the man probably hadn't really seen him when he was in town before, and if he had, Holt had shaved his beard since then. He pulled his hat down a little lower and nursed another beer as Pendleton sidled up to the bar. He threw down three whiskeys in rapid succession, then walked out, seemingly none the worse for the house whiskey.

Holt threw a couple coins on the table and left just a couple minutes later. The bulky form of Pendleton was still easy to follow from a distance. Holt's luck held when Pendleton entered a shack at the edge of town a few minutes later, slamming the door shut behind him. Holt slowed, then walked past the shack, glancing casually sideways as he did so. He was willing to bet no woman lived there. The place appeared to be just barely standing up. There were no flowers planted around the house anywhere, and Holt had the feeling he could pull one board loose just about any place he chose, and the whole shack would collapse. Whatever Pendleton was making from this horse rustling business, Holt concluded, it wasn't going into this place.

Holt turned and walked back past the house, headed for a boardinghouse he had passed on the way. He would be back in the morning to see what he could find in that shack.

Holt took his time over breakfast at the café the next morning. He finished his coffee leisurely and took a trip to the railroad office, sticking his head in the door just long enough to see that Pendleton was at work. He turned and meandered down the road to the shack where Pendleton had gone last night. He approached the door, looking slowing in both directions. There was no one in sight. He knocked loudly on the door and wasn't surprised when nobody answered. He tried the handle and found it open, so he went inside after glancing around one more time.

A small desk in the corner got his attention, but after shuffling through the papers for about five minutes, he found nothing of interest. He wondered if there might be a loose board in the floor with a hiding place under the house. He began tapping the boards in various places, without result. He stopped and glanced at the bed. It was simply a mattress resting on the floor, but on a hunch, he went over and lifted the edge of the mattress. He saw an envelope underneath and pulled it out.

There were no windows inside, and he didn't want to light the lantern. He moved instead to the back door of the shack and let himself out. Standing on what passed for a back porch, he reached inside and pulled out a single piece of paper. It read: Sam Starr. General delivery, Fort Smith, Arkansas. Beneath that he saw several lines of notes. They appeared to refer to horses sent through on the railroad at various dates in the past. Holt smiled to himself and pushed the paper back into the envelope. He went back inside, tossed the envelope back under the mattress and left by the back door, circling the house and proceeding back to the saloon for a premature celebration.

The next piece of the puzzle had fallen into place nicely, he reflected. Sam and Belle Starr were known to run an organization in The Nation that included fencing stolen horses, among other things. He felt certain he knew now where the horses were going.

Pendleton was a careful man by nature. He was saving his money from this rustling operation being run by a couple of old buddies from his childhood. After he had enough money, he planned to move to San Francisco and live in style. Meanwhile, he mumbled to himself for the hundredth time about the place he was living in as he opened the front door. He stopped immediately and looked around. Somebody had gone through the papers on the desk, he was sure. He looked quickly at the mattress on the floor in the corner. They had moved it. He stepped over and lifted it, reassuring himself that the envelopes and paper inside were still there.

Pendleton sat in a chair in the corner for a few minutes, thinking things over. Something just didn't feel right here. And, he reminded himself; he was a careful man. He picked up his hat, put it back on, and walked down to the telegraph office.

Sheriff Hutchins escorted the man who called himself Wes out the front door of the jail in Belton. Three days had passed since Ranger McKinnon had brought the man in, and he couldn't hold Wes any longer. He had contacted other sheriffs in the area, and no one knew anything about the man. There were no posters out on him. Hutchins strongly suspected Wes was up to no good, but he couldn't prove a thing.

He walked the prisoner out to the boardwalk in front of the jail and shook the bullets out of his gun, then handed it to him. Hutchins put the bullets in his pocket, then handed Wes his gun belt. "Ride out of town," he said shortly. "I don't want to see you around here no more." He turned, then turned back. "Oh, and Wes," he said, "don't even think about going back around the Maitlin ranch." He turned on his heel and went back in the jail.

Wes stood on the porch and watched Hutchins disappear inside the jail. He then walked over, mounted his horse, and rode slowly north toward the Maitlin ranch. He checked over his shoulder once in a while, but Hutchins wasn't following. Wes vowed he would settle that score he had with the big Ranger.

Chapter Ten
Gang from Scyene

I was lounging at the table after breakfast and I had to admit; I was enjoying it. Actually, I couldn't remember ever having lounged much, and I wasn't even sure I was doing it right. My family back in Tennessee was dirt-poor, and I had pretty much had to earn my keep, even when I was growing up. I ran the trap lines, hunted for food, and had to take care of the garden. I was lucky I'd gotten as much schooling as I had.

I looked up to find Jessie's eyes on me, a little smile on her face. She walked over and re-filled my coffee cup. "What are you thinking about?" she asked.

I hemmed and hawed for a while, then finally got around to answering what she asked. "Well," I said, "I've never been taken care of like this. I've got my big feet stowed away under your table all the time, and I... well, I feel like I should be doing something around here."

She sat down in the chair next to me and patted my arm. "Don't worry," she said. "The doctor said just one more day to do nothing but rest. He'll be back out tomorrow to look at you, and if he says it's OK, I'll have some light work you can do for a while."

I nodded. "Whatever the doc says," I said a little doubtfully. "As long as he doesn't talk about somebody shootin' my fool head off again..."

Jessie laughed and reached over to help me to my feet. "Would you like to go out to the back porch?" she asked. "You can sit out there in the sun. It's a pretty nice day. I can come and join you after I've done a few chores."

I agreed, and she walked me outside. As I was sitting down, I had a little dizzy spell and sat down a little faster than I'd planned on. Jessie reached out to steady me, concern on her face.

"Ash? You OK?"

I nodded. "I'm OK. I was just dizzy for a bit when I leaned over. OK now."

Jessie lingered over me for a moment. "You're sure?" I held onto her hand for just a second.

"I'm sure," I said. She looked at me for a moment, then leaned in and kissed me on the lips. I reached out and pulled her back in for another one, then she leaned back and we both smiled.

"I took advantage of you, didn't I?" she asked.

"Yep," I said. "I think you did. Took advantage of a poor, sick country boy, and I hope you make a reg'lar thing of it."

She laughed and leaned back. "That country boy accent of yours just comes and goes, doesn't it?"

Well, she had me there. She was on to me. I smiled a little sheepishly and waited while she went and got my gun belt. She brought it out and left it lying across my lap. Then she went back in the house. I leaned back in the chair and couldn't stop smiling.

The morning sun made me drowsy, and I found that I could tilt back in my chair and pull my hat down over my forehead to make myself comfortable. After a while, my eyelids became heavy, and I drifted off in the chair.

Some time later, a noise to my right brought me half-awake. I pushed my hat back and sat up. At the same time, I heard Jessie's brother Kyle shout my name as he came out of the barn. I registered the sound of his voice at the same time I saw someone stepping around the corner of the house, gun out.

I saw the man on my right stop and half-turn toward the barn when he heard my name shouted. The drowsiness fell away from me completely as I sat up and yanked my Colt.45 from the holster. He turned back toward me and our two shots sounded like one as we both fired at the same time. I heard his bullet whine past me and bury itself into the side of the house. My shot spun him around and he fell to his knees.

I didn't trust myself to stand, so I leaned forward, put both hands on the handle of the Colt and squeezed off two more shots as he tried to turn and bring his gun to bear. Both shots found their mark, and he pitched over backward and lay still in the grass.

I heard Jessie's shout from inside the house and heard her footsteps running toward the back door. "Hold it!" I shouted, keeping the gun trained on the form in the grass. When he didn't move after several seconds, I lowered the Colt. "OK," I said, "you can come out now."

Jessie and Iris both came from the house, and I could see Kyle moving in cautiously from the barn. "Help me up," I told Jessie, and she helped me get to my feet. I trained the gun on the man lying in the grass as she helped me slowly step down off the porch and walk over to him. I knelt and felt his wrist. When I was certain he was dead, I rolled him over onto his back. It was Wes, the man I had arrested a few days ago.

I heard a sharp intake of breath from Jessie, and I turned and looked up at her. "Is this the man who came here looking for work?" I asked. She nodded her head, then looked away from the dead body.

"Do you think he came here to get even with me for not hiring him?" she asked.

I rose slowly to my feet, and she stepped over and slid an arm around me to steady me. "No," I said. "I think it's more likely he came here to get even with me for arresting him and putting him in jail over in Belton."

Just then I heard a voice shout, "Hello! Ash?" and a man moved out slowly from the other corner of the house. I raised my gun instinctively, then relaxed when I realized I knew that voice very well. "Come on around Mike," I called out.

Mike Stone came around the corner and took in the scene of the dead man in the grass, me wobbling on my feet with my gun pointed at him, and the woman standing at my side, holding me up. His face broke into a grin.

"Well, Ash, I've always known you to be a little irritable, but you seem worse than usual today. And that's with a beautiful lady putting her arm around you, too." He made a reproachful noise that sounded like "ttsskkk" and shook his head. Jessie broke into a laugh and kept her arm right where it was.

I grinned and lowered my gun. "Mike Stone," I said, "I woulda said you're just jealous, but I know better. You showed up just in time. We could use a little help around here right now."

Milo Wills leaned back in his chair and stared out his office window on Houston Street in San Antonio, wondering how many of these people had voted for him in the last election. Whether any of these people had voted for him, there were enough people in the state who had voted for him to make him the newest Texas State Senator. He wasn't actually sure if he would have won fair and square without the votes he'd paid his "fixer" to get for him, but that really didn't matter. He'd won.

The sign out front said "Milo Wills, Attorney", and in fact it was his law office. He'd hired a kid named Barrett to do most of the legal work for him. He divided his time between trips to Austin and some work he did as a senator with another enterprise he was running that was far more profitable than the law office or the pay for being a senator. As a matter of fact, that third enterprise made almost all of his money for him. The other two just gave him a good public image and fed his ego.

Wills got up and crossed the floor to close his office door. He returned to his desk and pulled out a telegram he'd received from one of only two people in this world he'd chosen to trust. Well, he had to admit, there were three if he counted his "fixer", a man named Shaw. It wasn't that Shaw was honest or loyal, but Wills could always count on him to do what he was told to do if the money was right. He got things done, and he kept his mouth shut—that's what really mattered.

Wills returned to the telegram from his boyhood friend, Pendleton. Pendleton was an important part of that third business that made him a lot of money, but the news on that front wasn't good today. Wills scanned the telegram again:

> House here was broken into. Stop.
> Believe intruder might have found info on Belle S. Stop.
> Lance or the guy he hired might have gone into business for themselves. No new merchandise coming. Stop.

Wills tore the telegram into shreds and dropped it into a trash basket. He folded his hands behind his head and stared out the window again. He had set this up so that only three people knew he was running this operation. One was the guy he called his fixer, Shaw. The two of them had run a little cattle rustling operation for a while, stealing cows in South Texas and running them up the trail to Kansas. When he'd made enough money, he got respectable. Shaw would never be respectable, but he was useful, so Wills had brought him along.

The other two people were a man and a woman he had known since his childhood days in Scyene, Texas. Scyene, near Dallas, had been a pretty busy little town back in those days. The railroad had caused the town to boom for a while, but then folks in Scyene had refused to build a depot for the train, so now the railroad stopped in a place called Mesquite, and the town of Scyene was drying up. Wills suspected it would be gobbled up by another city one of these days.

While he was living there, though, Wills had made two friends who were very useful to him now. One was Pendleton, who had lived next door. When Wills had found out that Pendleton had gotten a job shipping things on the railroad, it hadn't been hard to persuade him to send a few stolen horses up the line to Kansas. Pendleton was greedy, but not too ambitious. Greed made a man do some crazy things sometimes, so Wills kept an eye on him. So far, he still trusted Pendleton.

The other friend from Scyene was a girl named Myra Maybelle Shirley. Folks called her May Shirley. May was friends with the Younger family, having grown up with them in Missouri, but Wills had steered clear of the Youngers, and now he was glad he had. Too many headlines in the newspaper. Wills like things to be quiet and profitable.

May Shirley had married a man named Reed, and they had moved around, mostly staying ahead of the law, from what he'd heard. Reed had gotten himself killed in a stagecoach robbery a few years later. There was a story that May had then married one of the Youngers for a few weeks, but he didn't really believe that story. Then, a few years ago, May had married a man named Sam Starr and moved to the Territory. Nowadays she was known as Belle Starr and they had themselves an operation in the northeast corner of the Territory, moving stolen horses and doing some bootlegging, mainly. It was perfect for Wills.

It had been a pretty sweet operation, so far. Only Pendleton and the Starrs knew who they were dealing with. Wills sent messages out to Wes, the scout, then to Holt and his boys, the horse thieves. The horses got passed along through somebody named Lance to Pendleton, who shipped them to Parsons, Kansas. The Starrs sent the money for the horses directly to him, and he distributed it. He was running the whole show while staying removed from it.

Until now. A scowl returned to his face and his stomach rumbled as he rummaged around in a desk drawer for some whiskey. All of this had a bad feel to it. First, the scout, Wes, hadn't reported in for more than a week. Then Wills had gotten word that the next expected robbery hadn't happened. He had thought there would be a few more horses headed north right now. And, to top it off, somebody had connected Pendleton with the Starrs and might be looking to move in on the operation.

He spilled the whiskey slightly as he poured a second glass and cursed softly to himself as he wiped off the desk with his hand and downed the drink. He had to decide what to do about this, and he probably needed to do it soon. He wasn't yet prepared to roll up the entire operation and move on to something else, but it sounded like he needed to make some changes. The first thing would be to make sure that nobody was taking the horses directly to Parsons,

Kansas, and selling them to the Starrs. He grabbed a piece of paper and began composing a telegram to Belle:

Belle:
I may have an employee going into business for himself. Stop. Name is Holt. Stop.
If he contacts you about buying horses, I want him to get a very unfriendly reception. Stop.
M

He set the telegram message aside and leaned back in the chair again. He would get Shaw to send that in a few minutes. There was something else still bothering him, but he couldn't quite put his finger on it. He reviewed in his mind how he had set up this operation. He sent messages directly to Wes, the scout, Holt, the horse thief, Pendleton, and Belle Starr. Only Pendleton and Starr knew who he was and could send him messages. He scowled into his whiskey glass and reached for a refill. Then he stopped with the whiskey bottle in mid-air.

He had no communication whatsoever with Lance, the go-between for Pendleton and Holt. Pendleton had no connection with Holt directly. So, he wondered, how did Holt know to break into Pendleton's house? Or were Lance and Holt working together, and it was Lance who had broken into Pendleton's house? He slammed the whiskey bottle down on the desk and rose to his feet. "Shaw!!!"

His voice echoed in the office, which he had never bothered to furnish, other than with the desk, desk chair, and one well-used side chair. Shaw, who usually lounged on a bench outside the office, came through the door. He had his usual disheveled look, and he wiped his mouth with a greasy sleeve from his buckskin jacket as he entered. His appearance slightly repulsed Wills, as usual, but he knew how, uh... effective Shaw was at what he did. The man had no scruples; he got things done, and he kept his mouth shut. A man like that was hard to find.

Wills picked up the telegram message and waved it impatiently in the air. "Take this down to the telegraph office and send it to Fort Smith—the usual place." Shaw grabbed the message and turned toward the door, but Wills stopped him. "Wait a minute, there's more. Go to Temple and find Pendleton. Tell him you want to know where to find Lance. Tell him you're going to watch Lance and make sure he isn't going into business for himself. Tell him if that's happening, you're going to straighten out Lance, and I'm not going to be happy."

Shaw nodded and moved to the door, then waited to see if Wills had anything else to say, triggering a fresh bout of temper. "Get going!" Wills shouted. He threw two gold pieces in Shaw's direction. "Make sure the telegraph operator keeps his mouth shut." Shaw nodded and left, glad to escape Will's foul temper. It was a good thing, he thought, that the pay was so good.

Ike rode into the Longhorn Cave hideout, still grimacing from time to time from the pain caused by the furrow across his back. He would carry that scar for the rest of his life to remind him of the rustling job at that ranch near Belton. He dismounted and tethered his horse, then walked into the cave. Slade could hear him coming, but didn't bother to get up. He kept one hand on his pistol and watched until he could see it was only Ike coming in. He leaned back against the cave wall, noting the rip across the back of Ike's jacket and the dried blood beneath it.

Slade watched as Ike rummaged around in his blankets until he found the flask he was looking for. "Didya get any horses?" Slade asked finally.

Ike cursed at length and took a very long pull from the flask. "Two," he said sullenly. "A mare and her colt. Didn't get the stallion we was after. Holt said we have to go back for him."

Slade digested that news for a while and watched as Ike finished the flask. "Well," he said finally, "we're going back for the stallion?"

Ike laid down carefully on his stomach and stretched out on the blankets. He didn't bother to give Ike an answer. There was time to think about that tomorrow. Slade stared at him and shrugged when he realized he wasn't going to get an answer to his question. He stretched out on his bedroll and soon was snoring even more loudly than Ike.

Chapter Eleven
Belle Starr

We sat around the kitchen table, enjoying the heat from the stove in the kitchen. Iris was baking, even though we'd all just had as much food as anybody could possibly put down for dinner. That included me, and that was saying something. Kyle moved out to the porch to keep watch. The stallion and remaining best mares and colts were still in the corral behind the house, and none of us felt sure there wouldn't be another try at rustling the stock we still had out there.

Stone told us about his meeting with McDonald, and we filled him in on the robbery here just a couple days ago, what I had learned about the scout Wes, and how he had tried to hire on at ranches before the robberies happened. We agreed that he probably hadn't been involved in the actual thefts. He seemed to have been sending information to somebody. Then he moved on before the rustlers moved in. We had been hoping there would be something in his pockets or in a saddlebag, telling us who he was working with, but we'd been disappointed there. We found nothing at all to help us.

When we were done, he told us about the racetrack just off the Chisholm Trail up north, and how he had seen a horse that might have been one of the rustled animals. He told us he thought the horses were being moved out of state on the railroad, where they were maybe being sold as race horses or breeding stock.

Stone got up and walked over to the burlap bag he always carried with him when he was out travelling. He rummaged around in it for a bit, then came back with a map which he spread out on the table. I leaned in to take a look. It was a map of the central part of Texas. I could see Austin in the middle and Dallas and Ft. Worth on the north side. It ran down a little below San Antonio at the bottom. Stone asked Jessie for a pencil and she went to get him one.

When she came back with the pencil, Stone began drawing circles on the map, and explained that McDonald had a map like this back in his office. The circles, he said, were where he knew there had been horses stolen—horses like the ones taken from Jessie's ranch, not just random rustling of cowboy ponies. I leaned in and saw that he had drawn circles around Lampasas, Belton, Salado, and a place just a little north of San Antonio.

Jessie moved a lantern to the table as darkness fell outside. "Were the robberies one after the other, moving up or down this half-circle?" she asked hopefully.

Stone shook his head slowly. "Nope," he said. "They're too smart for that, I guess. They've hopped from north to south and back again. This probably can't tell us where they're going to strike next. Here's what I'm hoping." He took the pencil and drew a big circle, using the robberies on the map as a guideline. When he had finished, there was a circle around the middle of Texas, with Austin roughly in the middle.

"What I'm hoping," he continued, "is that this gang is operating somewhere near the middle of the circle. Not exactly the middle, I'm sure, maybe a little north or a little south, but maybe they're coming from a hideout somewhere in the middle, like spokes on a wagon wheel. They steal the horses, hide them somewhere for a while, alter the brands maybe, then load them on a rail car and sell 'em somewhere up north. Out of Texas, probably."

I stared at the map, nodding my head slowly. "That could be," I agreed, "but that circle covers a whole lot of ground. How would you suggest we start lookin' for 'em? I wasn't in any shape to trail them after they took the mare and her colt from here. Does anybody have an idea which direction they head after they rustle the horses?"

Stone shrugged in frustration. "Nobody's got a good idea," he admitted. "Somewhere toward the middle of that circle is probably fair to say." He drummed his fingers on the table for a minute, then looked up at me.

"You're an excellent tracker, Ash. How would you hide tracks and keep from leaving a trail? Just in general, I mean."

I sat back in the chair, distracted for a minute by the apple pie I saw Iris lifting out of the oven. Jessie followed my gaze, laughed, and got up to get me a piece of it. Stone just rolled his eyes and waited for me to answer his question.

"Water," I mumbled, half to myself. "Water is good for covering tracks. You wait and move them after it rains, or you splash through water in streams and rivers." I looked back at the map. "There's a lot of rivers and streams there. I don't know where I would start."

Stone nodded, then drew a line north and south on the map. "This is the rail line for the Missouri, Kansas, and Texas Railroad," he said. "Most folks call it the KATY. Don't get too far away from the KATY rails. They still have to move the horses out of here and sell them."

Stone got up and moved back to the window, staring at the horses in the corral in the fading light. "I think I want to start checking at the railroad stations around here," he said over his shoulder. "I'm going to start here with the closest stop in Temple and work my way north. I'm going to see if I can get any clues about how the horses are loaded and moved, and where they might be going."

He turned around and came back to the table. "How long before you're up and around, Ash? Any idea?"

I glanced over at Jessie and Iris. "I'll know more tomorrow," I said. "The doc is supposed to come back and take another look at me tomorrow." I paused. "You want me to try to figure where the horses are held until they go to the railroad? Maybe I can get working on that in a few days. Maybe there are a couple tracks still out there after they hit this place."

"That's what I'm hoping," Stone said. He stared at my empty plate. "I could have sworn there was a piece of pie on that plate," he mumbled. He looked at Iris. "You're never going to get those enormous feet out from under your table, you know."

Iris dished up a piece of pie for Mike and pulled my plate over to give me another piece. I protested just enough to sound polite. Iris ignored me and loaded me up with seconds, just like I'd planned it. "That's just fine, Mr. Stone," she said. "We enjoy having your friend at this table."

Holt halted near the edge of the town of Waco. It was dusk. There were few horses entering town, and for that matter, few on the streets of Waco. He was getting very tired of building makeshift corrals to hide the mare and colt while he tried to make arrangements for getting them out of Texas. He hesitated, then thought how much he would like to put the horses into a stable and head on down to a pub. He dismounted and checked the altered brands. They seemed to be pretty well healed over. He abruptly re-mounted and proceeded into town. He paused when he saw a livery stable.

There was an old man sweeping up near the stalls, paying no attention to Holt. Making his decision, Holt led the mare and colt into the stables. The old man looked up, chewing on a piece of straw, waiting for Holt to say something. He glanced at the horses with no expression on his face.

Holt swept a hand, including all three horses in his gesture. "How much for all three for one night?" he demanded.

The old man removed the straw from his mouth, barely glanced at the horses, and said, "One dollar."

Holt started to protest the price, which seemed a little high, then decided he didn't want to say or do anything that might cause the old man to remember him. He simply shrugged, dug a coin out of his pocket, and handed over the reins.

Moving out of the livery stable, he began walking the several blocks toward the train station. He paid for his ticket first and sized up the situation while he did so. He hoped to slip the stolen horses onto the train without paying the agent. He stepped up to the booth and bought a ticket for himself to Parsons, Kansas, on the morning train.

Moving into the train yard, Holt searched the area, his eyes resting on a short, seedy-looking man leading a horse away from one of the train cars. Holt approached the man, then stepped in front of him, tossing two silver dollars in the air and catching them as the man stopped and stared at him.

"I've got three horses I want to put on the train tomorrow morning," Holt said casually. The man watched the silver coins for a moment, then nodded toward the ticket window.

"You kin buy passage for yer horses over there," he announced, watching Holt carefully, then looking back at the silver dollars.

"I don't really want to pay over there," Holt said smoothly. "I was hoping maybe you could help me. These silver dollars are getting a little heavy in my pocket."

The man's face broke into a gap-toothed smile very briefly, then he looked around. "If'n you was to have those horses here at about eight o'clock in the morning, I could prob'ly hep you with that," he muttered in an undertone.

Holt passed him the two dollars. "We understand each other," he said. I'll have them here in the morning."

Holt was up early and brought the mare and her colt to the train yard. He handed off the two stolen horses, along with his own horse, and watched as the handler loaded them on to a railroad car. Satisfied, he went to the telegraph office. He had a message to send before he was ready to board the train himself.

Holt took his time over the message he wanted to send to Sam Starr, or Belle Starr. He wasn't sure exactly who he was dealing with, but it didn't matter. He just needed to establish a way to sell horses in the Territory. He had decided he didn't want to try to take over any business that The Boss, whoever that was, had going on here. He knew that might be pretty dangerous. He would just try to set up a connection for himself, selling directly.

After several messages that he tore up, Holt finally decided on a direct approach:

Arriving in Parsons, Kansas on Tuesday the 3rd. Stop.
Will have two fine horses. Good for racing. Stop.
Arabian bloodlines. Stop.
Meet me at the train if interested. Stop.
Ask for Holt. Stop.

He read the message over several times, then had it sent out. Satisfied, he boarded the train and looked out the window as they passed through the central part of Texas. In a couple of days, he hoped he would have found someone to fence all the horses he could steal. He tipped his hat down over his eyes, leaned back, and drifted off to sleep.

Sam Starr looked down at the two telegrams in his hand. They had come together, delivered from Ft. Smith to the saloon operated by the Starrs. They had opened the saloon near the ranch they called Younger's Bend in the Territory. A fight broke out in the saloon and he paused, watching to make sure nothing else was going to get broken. They were still cleaning up from the last fight in here. When he saw one fighter go down and pass out on the floor, he returned his attention to the telegrams.

He frowned when he saw that the first had come from Belle's old friend from Texas. She always insisted on dealing with him personally. The frown deepened when he saw the second message. Things seemed to be getting complicated, and Sam liked things to be simple. He saw Belle watching him from across the saloon. She walked over, eyebrows raised, and looked at the messages in his hand. He handed them over and waited.

Belle read them, then read them again. She folded up both messages and tucked them into a pocket. "Send Victorio to Parsons," she said simply. "Have him take care of this." She stopped and turned before walking away. "Have him bring the horses here."

When she had turned and left the saloon, Sam Starr allowed the scowl to deepen across his face. He passed a hand across his forehead. Parsons, Kansas, was a long way to go in the first place. The railroad was building a station in Eufaula now, so maybe that would make things easier if they had to keep dealing with this guy Wills. He sighed and looked around the bar for Victorio.

When he found Victorio leaning on the bar, an empty glass in front of him, Starr motioned to him, then turned and went outside. He waited for Victorio to catch up to him. Starr handed him a few coins, then leaned forward to whisper. "Go to Parsons," he said. "There will be a man on Tuesday's train named Holt who will want to sell us two horses. Kill Holt and take the horses. Bring them here."

Starr didn't wait for a response. He walked away and went back into the saloon. Maybe, he thought, the two horses would be worth all this trouble, after all. He was tiring of keeping Belle happy when she insisted on dealing with Wills.

Stone observed the ticket agent, then repeated his question. "Has there been somebody come through here in the last couple days, wanting to ship a sorrel mare and a colt, and maybe go north along with the horses?" The agent who had given his name as Pendleton, was making a production of cleaning out a drawer behind the window where he sat. He hadn't made eye contact since Stone had walked up to ask him questions.

Pendleton's hands stopped moving when Stone asked about the horses, then went back to re-arranging the drawer. He glanced up briefly, seeming to take a moment to think about the question. "No," he said clearly. "Nobody came through shipping a mare and colt. Why?" He stopped and waited for the answer.

"Horse rustlers," Stone stated flatly. "Shipping stolen horses, taken from a ranch near here. You're sure?"

Irritation showed in Pendleton's face. And maybe, Stone thought, a bit of fear. "Of course, I'm sure," he said brusquely. "Anything else?"

Stone shook his head slowly, still watching Pendleton's face. Something told him it might be worthwhile to come back here and keep an eye on this one. He reached into his pocket for a coin. "Ticket to Waco," he said.

Riding the train north, Stone began to re-evaluate his strategy. He wasn't likely to get a corrupt ticket agent to confess to shipping stolen horses. He might do better by trying to find somebody who had seen the horses or loaded the horses. Plus, he still didn't know what the destination might be. Where were they actually going? He had found one of the horses near the northern border of Texas. They might go farther north than that.

By the time the train had chugged into Waco, Stone had decided to stay in town for a day or two, asking questions and deciding just how far north he was willing to go in pursuit of the stolen horses. He waited for his horse to be unloaded from the train car, then walked him down to a livery stable he'd seen as they pulled into town.

The old man at the stables took his horse and his money without comment, and Stone turned and started for the street. He stopped and turned back. It didn't seem likely, but he might as well ask. "Did anybody come in here in the last few days with a sorrel mare and a colt?" he asked.

The old man forked some hay down for Stone's horse, taking his time, then leaned over and spit. He straightened up slowly. "Aye," he said, "sorrel mare an' her colt, mebbe two days ago. Somebody'd been workin' over them brands, if you ask me." He whistled tunelessly and moved past Stone, heading for the chair he'd been in when Stone arrived.

"Hang on," Stone said, "what do you mean working over the brands? They'd been altered?"

The old man took a seat, letting out a little grunting noise as he did so. "Aye, they'd been worked over, pretty recent, I'd say. It were a Circle M brand, but I'd say it were a Rocking M not too long before. Pretty sloppy job with the runnin' iron, I'd say," he added scornfully. He picked up a stick and a knife and began whittling. He stopped and looked up at Stone, taking in the badge on his chest. "Was he a rustler?"

"Probably." Stone knelt down beside the old man. "What did this guy look like? Tall, short, what color hair?"

"Yeller hair, it was." The old man squinted at the afternoon sun. "Kinda short. Pretty dang grumpy, if'n you ask me. Tiny little boots. Tiny. Big ole' bruise on his jaw. I'd say somebody punched him good." He resumed the whittling and the tuneless whistling. Stone left the livery stable at a trot, headed for the train station again.

A few quick questions to the station ticket agent told Stone everything he needed to know. A short, blonde man with a nasty yellowing bruise on his jaw had bought a ticket for Parsons, Kansas two days ago. The agent didn't recall that the man was shipping horses, and he had given his name as Smith, which probably didn't mean anything.

Stone was set back for a few minutes when the agent said that "Smith" hadn't paid to ship any horses north. Then he remembered what the old man at the livery stable had said about the altered brands on the horses. He looked around the train yard and saw a man unloading cargo from one car. He approached the man, who took one look at Stone's badge and ducked around the train car, trotting in the other direction. Stone didn't bother to chase him. He had a pretty good idea how the stolen horses could have gotten on the train.

Chapter Twelve
Death in Kansas

Sheriff Hutchins showed up at the house not much past daybreak. He said he wanted to take the corpse back to town. He said he would get it buried proper. I'm guessing he also wanted folks to know, come election time, that he didn't allow horse rustling around here. That was OK with me. He tossed the body into a wagon he'd brought along, then came up to join Jessie and me on the porch.

Jessie handed him a cup of coffee, and he warmed his hands around the cup for a minute. "You folks doing OK, now?" he asked. "Do you think they're done rustling horses here?"

Jessie and I look at each other, neither one of us feeling confident about the answer. "They didn't get the stallion," I said, "and I'm guessing they wanted him most of all. He was the biggest prize around here."

Hutchins nodded that he understood and took a long, loud slurp of his coffee. "I've got a deputy I can spare in a couple days," he offered. "He's lookin' into something for me out east of town right now, but I could send him out when he gets back."

We agreed, and Hutchins finished up his coffee, then drove the wagon out of the yard. As he left, Doc Linden rode in, stopping to exchange a few words with the sheriff. He rode on up to the porch and dismounted. I touched my hand to the bandage on my head, hoping he would tell me I could go back to work.

Doc climbed up on to the porch, glancing back at the wagon being driven away by the sheriff. "Well," he said, turning back around to look at me. "I guess there's no shortage of folks wanting to shoot your fool head off." He softened the words with a chuckle when he finished.

"I'm popular," I agreed.

He unwound the bandage on my head, turning me to get a better look in the morning light, and making a few noises—I had no idea what they meant. He moved his hand back and forth in front of me, watching my eyes. "Any headaches?" he asked abruptly.

"I've had several," I admitted, "but yesterday and so far, today, my head doesn't hurt anymore." I looked at him hopefully.

He took his watch out of his pocket and glanced at it, then tossed it up and down while he took one more look at me. "OK," he said finally. "You can get up and around, do some light work for a few days. If you still feel good after that, consider yourself healed up. The wound looks good," he added.

He stopped after stepping down from the porch and looked back at me, then at Jessie. "Nice to see somebody helping to look after this little family," he said. He glanced at both of us again. "Might make a good full-time job for somebody. I'm just sayin'..." He chuckled at the quick blush that appeared on Jessie's face, mounted up, and rode out.

"Well," said Jessie, the blush on her face fading away. "I told you the doc actually likes you." She took both my hands to help lift me up from the chair. "Come on," she said. "I promised I would put you to work when the doc said it's OK."

I trailed after her into the house. I didn't seem to have anything to say, but that silly grin was back on my face.

Holt folded his coat and pressed it up against the side of the train car. He was used to being out in the open; being confined in this train car for two days was getting the best of him. He hadn't gotten a lot of sleep, and he'd had too much time to think about things. He reviewed in his mind what was bothering him the most.

He didn't want to cross the Starrs, and he didn't know what the connection was between whoever had been sending him the telegrams and the Starrs. Whoever The Boss was, he seemed like somebody who didn't get his hands dirty. Holt knew he could handle that. The Starrs, though, ran a pretty big operation in the Territory, from what he'd heard, and he didn't want to cross them. Besides, if they didn't buy the horses, where was he going to get good money for them?

The train swayed suddenly around a bend, and Holt swore under his breath. He didn't feel like taking this ride very often; he would have to set up a way to send the horses and get paid without traipsing off to Kansas every time. He reassured himself that his plan was a good one and leaned back up against the train window. Sheer fatigue was taking over, and he felt his eyelids rolling shut. This was going to work out, he told himself...

The train's whistle brought him wide awake, and he saw that the sun was dropping in the west—he must have been asleep for several hours. He turned and saw the conductor coming down the aisle. He waved his hand to flag the man down. "Where are we?" he blurted out.

The conductor paused only to glance at him before moving on. "Parsons, Kansas," came the reply. "We'll be stopping here for about an hour. Going to load some wood for the engine and let those off who are stopping here." He turned and moved on.

Holt jumped up and grabbed his bag from the rack above him. He hopped off the car as soon as it stopped moving, then trotted down to claim the mare and colt after he had them unloaded. A quick glance told him they had survived the trip without a problem. He claimed his own horse next and began leading all three animals away from the tracks. He looked around and saw a man in leather breeches and vest watching him closely. He paused and took in the long scar across the man's face, and the hair tied off and falling halfway down his back. This, he thought, could be somebody sent by the Starrs. He turned slightly and headed toward the man, who was clearly sizing him up.

Victorio watched silently as the stranger approached him. A quick glance at the mare and colt convinced him that this was the man wanting to sell horses. He turned his unblinking stare on the man himself. Victorio noted that he was a small man with two tied-down guns at his hips. He knew instantly that this man prided himself on these guns. He would never challenge Victorio to a fist fight, and wouldn't rely on a knife. Victorio glanced down at his own gun, hanging from a rawhide strip around his neck. He was surprisingly good with the pistol, but he would always prefer to use the knife inserted through a leather band around his waist.

Victorio was the son of an Apache father and a white woman who had been carried away captive by the Apaches when she was just a girl. Victorio had grown up with his tribe in Arizona, but he was smart enough to know that their way of life was ending there. He had known enough of the white man and his ways to leave the Apaches and travel to the Territory. He had become useful to the Starrs for just this kind of work. He knew what to do.

The small man with the two guns stopped in front of him. "I have two nice horses here," he said, studying Victorio's face. "Maybe you could use a couple horses like these."

Victorio watched him, his face remaining impassive. He nodded almost imperceptibly. "Maybe I could," he said. He walked around the mare, running his hands over her shoulder and looking at her teeth. "I need to ride her before I can know if we will buy her." He glanced over his shoulder and pointed toward some open pasture land, away from the railroad and town. He had to get away from the town to do his job.

The stranger hesitated, looking doubtfully in the direction indicated by Victorio, who felt himself growing impatient. He lifted the hackamore rope in his hand. "You can hold my horse while I ride." He watched as the stranger's expression gradually changed from suspicious to one of agreement. Holt motioned for Victorio to lead the way.

Victorio moved ahead, glancing back only occasionally to be sure the stranger was following. He walked for several minutes, then veered around a stand of cottonwood trees. He felt sure the trees would block the view from the town. He took a few more steps, involuntarily touching the handle of the knife at his side. Now, he decided, was the time...

Holt had a bad feeling as soon as he started talking to the man with the scar on his face. That it was somebody who worked for the Starrs, he had no doubt. The man was part-Indian; he was sure, and he looked like a man who could handle himself in a fight. Holt had no intention of getting into a fight. At the moment, he just wanted to sell the horses and get away with his hide intact. He forced himself to look as relaxed as possible and followed the man out of town.

The farther they went, away from the view of anyone in town, the more he glanced back and felt his tension rising. They skirted around a stand of cottonwood trees, and he knew no one could see them now. Then he saw the man's hand touch the knife. He released the reins he held in his right hand and rested the hand on one of his pistols. When the stranger stopped and whirled, Holt drew the gun and fired point-blank.

Starr's man wore a completely startled expression when the first shot struck him in the chest; he dropped the knife and staggered backwards. Holt's second shot went straight through the heart. By the time the stranger hit the ground, Holt was looking around, deciding what to do with the body. He led the mare and colt back to the cottonwood trees and tethered them, then did the same with his own horse, which had run off only a short distance. He shooed the dead man's horse away and ran him off a short distance. Then he dragged the body under the trees. It would have to do. He didn't want to stay out here any longer.

Back at the train station, there was only one employee for the railroad. He sold tickets, loaded and unloaded baggage, helped load firewood and did whatever else he had to do. He had made some nice extra money for the last year or so, by unloading some horses that didn't seem to belong to anybody, and holding them for people he was pretty sure were fencing stolen horses.

He had watched the exchange in the train yard and was pretty sure they had stolen the mare and colt. Plus, he recognized the guy who had waited for the train. He'd delivered several horses to this man before. When he heard a couple gunshots and saw the train passenger coming back with the mare and colt, with no sign of the man who had waited for the train, he had a decision to make. Did he keep his mouth shut or not?

Greed won out. He dashed off a telegram to the man in Temple named Pendleton. Maybe it would be worth a few extra dollars. He already knew what he would do with the extra money.

Two days later, Holt was getting more than just a little worried. Because the Chisum Trail ran to the west of here and Parsons was such a small town, he had had no luck in selling the horses on his own. Horses of the kind he was selling were mostly good for outlaws who needed the speed or cowboys who liked to race them, and there was a shortage of both around here. Mostly he had just looked for a place to hide out for a couple of days, hoping that any danger to him after the shooting would die down.

He'd spent the time camping in a small grove of trees west of town, close to a stream. January nights got a little too cold for him here, but he kept a fire going. It wasn't really the cold that got him moving. He knew that before too long, word was likely to get back to the Starr outfit that their man was dead. He didn't need to be hanging around Parsons, Kansas, when that happened.

On the third morning, he decided. He would go back to Texas, stopping at Dennison on the northern border. He would get the best price he could for the horses, whatever that was, then go back down to Longhorn Cave and lie low for a while. This would blow over eventually, then he would figure out what to do next. He gathered the horses and rode back into Parsons, leading the mare and the colt. He bought passage for himself and the horses back to Texas. There was only one man working the depot, and Holt ignored his curious stares. He needed to get home. When the train arrived, he boarded and heaved a sigh of relief.

The agent at the train station watched as the southbound train pulled away. He checked the watch in his pocket. Two hours until the next train. He had time to send another telegram.

Stone chafed at the delay in getting to Parsons. The locomotive had broken down yesterday, and they had spent almost a full day sidelined just south of Ft. Worth. Stone worried that whatever was going to happen with those horses in Parsons had already happened. He knew there was very little chance of recovering them if they had been moved already.

On the other hand, sitting on the train for nearly a day had given him a chance to think, and Stone had a gift for analyzing things. His mind kept returning to the question of why the destination picked by the horse thief was Parsons. It was a tiny little stop on the route. If the thief was looking to fence the horses, it seemed a very unlikely destination. And yet, he reasoned, there had to be a reason.

When the engine had finally been repaired and the train had started to move yesterday evening, it had hit him like a thunderbolt. One of the biggest operations for fencing stolen horses, among other things, was in northeastern Oklahoma. The woman now known as Belle Starr, along with her husband Sam, were known to buy and dispose of stolen horses. What if the horses stolen in Texas had found their way to the Territory, or for that matter, places north and east of there? The Starrs probably had that kind of reach. It fit together in Stone's mind.

By the time the train stopped in Dennison to load up firewood, Stone had reviewed in his mind what he knew about the Starrs. Sam Starr was native to Oklahoma, as far as Stone knew, but Belle had Texas ties. The Rangers had kept up with Belle, although she was now living and working entirely in the Territory. Stone knew that Belle, or May Shirley, as she was mostly known then, had grown up in a town near Dallas called Scyene. Maybe the Texas connection was there?

Stone stared out at the train yard in Dennison and decided to go out and stretch his legs. They had another forty-five minutes before moving out. He thrust his hands in his pockets and began walking vigorously, though aimlessly, around the train yard. The Younger brothers had come from Scyene, but they had gone to prison a few years ago after that bank robbery in Minnesota.

After about fifteen minutes of walking and turning things over in his mind, Stone decided it might be worth going over to Scyene when he came back from Parsons. He could do a little checking around over there and see if he came up with anything from Belle Starr's background that might tie her to the horse rustling in Texas.

Stone turned to re-board his train, vaguely aware of activity from a train that had arrived from the north. Passengers were getting off the train and baggage and horses were being offloaded. Stone glanced over and stopped in his tracks. There was a man across the way with sandy-blonde hair, standing a little on the short side, leading three horses away from one of the baggage cars. There was a sorrel horse and a colt. It all fit the descriptions he had been given. As Stone started to move toward them, the man glanced over, then spun and began moving in the other direction.

Milo Wills stared at the telegram he held in his hand, his stomach turning over as he read it. He set the telegram on his desk, then forced himself to sit down and think calmly. The telegram, from Pendleton, told him that the horse rustler, Holt, had killed Belle Starr's man in Parsons. A few days later, he had gotten back on the KATY railroad train, along with the rustled horses, to return to Texas. It was, it forced Wills to admit, the worst news he could have received today.

He had no doubt that the Starrs would have revenge in mind when they found out their man was dead. They might even blame him. He had to do something about this before the Starrs found out. More than that, he had to wrap up this operation now and walk away. It had become too dangerous. He needed to get Holt out of the picture immediately. Pendleton, he still felt he could trust. The man that worked for Pendleton, though, Lance somebody—he had to be taken out of the way too.

Wills opened the door to his office and motioned to Shaw, his fixer, who was lounging in a chair outside. As soon as Shaw stepped in, Wills handed him three gold pieces. He didn't bother to sit down, or even to step away from the door. "Pendleton had a man working for him, first name Lance. He isn't useful to me anymore. Find out what you need to know about him from Pendleton, then make him go away. After that, go to Longhorn Cave. Find out who is there and if they have any horses there."

Shaw took the gold pieces, a smile touching the corners of his mouth. This was what he did best. He put on his hat and went outside to mount up.

That took care of one problem. Wills sat down behind his desk again and stared out the window. What to do about Holt? It occurred to him that with Lance out of the way, there was no possible way for anyone to tie Holt back to him. He drummed his fingers on the desk and turned a couple of possibilities over in his mind, then rejected each one as being too dangerous.

Suddenly, his fingers stopped drumming, and a smile spread slowly over his face as he looked out the window. Maybe the Texas Rangers would like to know a little about a horse rustler named Holt. They could do his work for him. With any luck, there would be a shootout and they would kill Holt. Even if they just arrested him, the Starrs would avoid trying to come after him for revenge. Too dangerous for them, he mused. The more he thought about it, the better he liked his plan.

He swung around to his desk and picked up his pen to compose a telegram. What was the name of that Rangers captain he had met in Austin earlier this year? He frowned and stared at the opposite wall. McDonald! That was it. He grabbed a piece of paper and composed an anonymous telegram for Captain McDonald. When he had finished, he swung around and looked out the window. Shaw was already gone, so he rose and picked up his hat. He could send this telegram himself.

Chapter Thirteen
What Goes Around...

Holt collected his horses at the Dennison station as quickly as he could, feeling like he was being watched. He knew it was probably too soon for the Starrs to have caught up with him, but he was getting more and more jumpy. The thought had struck him on the way down on the train that maybe somebody there in Parsons was in touch with Sam or Belle Starr. He told himself that wasn't likely, but he wasn't entirely convinced. Despite the cool temperatures on this winter day, he felt a trickle of sweat run down the back of his neck.

He led the horses away, trying to get his bearings. He wasn't sure which direction he wanted to go, but decided it would be enough for right now just to get away from the train station and the town of Dennison. It was a little unusual to see a man leading two horses and a colt, and he felt conspicuous any time he drew a second glance from anybody. It wasn't helping, he admitted to himself, that he was returning those curious glances with hostile stares.

He resolved to look down and not draw eye contact, but the sound of another train arriving and unloading across the yard caused him to look up. The sight of metal flashing in the sun drew his eyes, and he stopped his sweeping glance to look back at what he'd seen. His stomach began to churn when he realized he was looking at a badge. He froze momentarily, then quickened his pace to reach a couple of outbuildings at the edge of the train yard. He turned the corner, looking back over his shoulder as he did so. The man with the badge was following.

Holt fought down the panic as he broke into a trot, urging the horses to keep up. His gaze swept left and right. He was having trouble deciding what to do. A small voice inside him kept telling him the lawman wasn't really following him; he needed to calm down. The rest of him didn't seem to listen to the small voice. He saw a short hitching rail outside the final of the outbuildings he was passing. On impulse, he trotted over and tied up the horses.

He turned and retraced his steps, forcing himself to calm down. If the lawman was still behind him, the man would probably just walk past him and keep going. He probably wouldn't even realize it was the same guy he'd just seen with the three horses. Holt continued to talk to himself while his heart pounded faster. His mouth felt increasingly dry.

The man turned the corner, and Holt could see the badge again. He took a couple more steps in that direction, but the guy with the badge had stopped walking, and he was staring directly at Holt. Reflex and pure panic set in. Holt's right hand swept down for his gun. He cleared the holster and a mixture of relief and excitement swept over him. He would shoot the lawman and get out of town. Problem solved.

A blow hammered him in the stomach, and he staggered back, staring down in confusion. He could feel pain in his shoulder, too, and he wasn't holding his gun any more. He stared at the blood pooling on the ground and wondered who had been shot. He looked up to see the man with the badge, holding a gun in his right hand and stepping toward him. Holt reached down for his other gun with his left hand and tried to claw it free. He never registered the third shot that struck him. He was dead when he landed on his back in the alley.

Mike Stone stood in the alleyway, gun still in hand, watching for any sign of movement from the man he had followed around the corner. When several seconds passed and he saw no movement, he approached the man slowly, gun still drawn. As he came closer, he put the gun back in the holster. There was no chance the man was still alive. When Stone heard footsteps coming from behind him, he removed his badge and held it in the air.

"Texas Ranger," he announced. "Do you have a sheriff in town?" When he heard a voice telling him they would find the sheriff, he nodded and knelt beside the body. He didn't recognize the man, but he hadn't really expected to. His eyes travelled down and stopped when he saw the boots. They were exceptionally small. He looked around at the prints left in the dust of the alley. He felt sure he had found the man who had ambushed Red.

Remembering that he had started to follow this man when he saw the three horses, including a colt, Stone stood and walked farther down the alley. He saw three horses tethered at a rail at the side of the last building. He walked over and inspected the brands on the mare and the colt. Someone had altered them; he could see that clearly. He untied the stolen horses and walked back toward the corpse, where he saw the sheriff standing and waving people away from the body.

Stone approached, introduced himself, and asked the sheriff if he would take charge of the body, explaining that the man was a horse thief and had very likely been the killer of a fellow Ranger. The sheriff agreed and gave orders for somebody to bring him a wagon. Stone then led the horses away, quickening his pace when he heard the train whistle. He needed to get his bag and his own horse off the train before it left. There was no need to continue on to Kansas.

Stone arranged for the stolen horses to be sent to Temple, then moved on from the train station to the telegraph office. There, he composed a lengthy telegram to Captain McDonald. He explained about the shootout and the death of the man who had the stolen horses. He also explained why he believed the dead man had been Red's killer. Finally, he told the captain why he wanted to go to Scyene. He sent the telegram, then went to a café nearby. He would wait for a reply from McDonald.

McDonald sat in the boarding room he used when he had to sit at a desk in Austin. These days, he reflected with some frustration, that happened more often than he wanted. He longed for the days when he had spent his time in the saddle. Unable to get himself started on a report to the governor, he went over to the telegraph office and check for messages. He found two waiting for him when he arrived. The first was a message from Mike Stone. He dashed off a response, telling Stone to proceed to Scyene. He made a mental note to let the governor know that Red's killer had been killed in a gunfight with Stone.

The second note caused his eyes to widen in surprise. He returned to the desk with the message and handed it across to the clerk. "Can you tell me where this was sent from?" he asked.

The clerk glanced at it briefly. "I can tell you where this one came from," came the quick answer. "The operator puts his initials on them. This came from San Antonio."

Surprised at how easy that had been, McDonald started to leave, then turned back. "Can you tell me where in San Antonio I can find this office?"

The clerk glanced at McDonald's badge, then typed out a message. He waited a few minutes for the reply, then picked it up and read it. "Commerce Street, near the river," he said.

McDonald, who had never been to San Antonio despite his years of service as a Ranger, stayed by the desk, debating his next question. Finally, he asked, "Which river would that be?"

The clerk didn't pause or look up as he typed out a new message. "San Antonio River, sir." McDonald thanked him and let himself out quietly.

Back at his boarding room office, McDonald sipped from a fresh cup of coffee and stared thoughtfully out the window. Clearly, whoever had sent this message was unaware of what had just happened up in Dennison. He spread the message out on his desk and read it again.

To McDonald. Stop.
A horse rustler named Holt is travelling on the KATY

Railroad with two stolen horses - mare and colt. Stop. Headed south from Parsons Ks. two days ago. Stop. Believed to have killed a man in Parsons. Stop.

The message didn't say who the sender was, of course. The part about coming south with stolen horses had turned out to be true. There were a few questions that came to mind. Who sent the message was an obvious one. Beyond that, why did this person want the horse rustler caught? If it was an honest citizen who wanted to see the rustler caught, why not identify themselves? And who was the man killed in Kansas, if that part was true?

Too many questions to deal with right now, he told himself. The first thing to do was to send somebody to that telegraph office in San Antonio and see what they could find out about the sender. McDonald frowned as he considered who he could send. He didn't really have anybody to spare right now. Then a smile crossed his face as he thought of an answer that would solve two problems. He could send himself. He could get out from behind this desk and get back to doing what he liked about this job.

A return to light work suited me just fine. I spent a day or two repairing some fences alongside Kyle, then spent another day checking on the horses and the small herd of cows with Jessie. It was too cold to move them to the higher pastures at the north end of the property, but Jessie and I decided it wasn't too cold for a picnic alongside the stream cutting through those pastures. Iris had packed the lunch for us with a knowing smile on her face. We spread out a blanket beside the stream and Jessie began unpacking the lunch.

"My mom likes you, you know," she told me. There was a teasing smile on her face.

"Of course she does," I said, leaning back with a smug smile on my face. "Mothers always love me." I settled back on the blanket and dropped the smug part of my smile. "I just have to do a better job of getting the daughters to love me."

"Daughters?" Jessie said, pausing mid-way through the unpacking. "Daughters? Just how many of those daughters do you plan on getting to love you?"

Well, that hadn't come out quite right. "Daughter," I said. "I just need one daughter." I leaned past Jessie, reaching for the cookies in the basket, and got a playful slap on my hand.

"That's for dessert," she said, leaning into me as she reached to put a plate of chicken on the blanket. It seemed to me that she stayed that way, leaning into me longer than necessary while she re-arranged the chicken on the plate. Me, I wasn't complaining.

"Did you have any mother and daughter in particular in mind?" she asked. "I'm just curious. Is this a long list or a short list?"

Jessie turned and looked at me, one eyebrow arched. I started to say something, got a little tongue-tied and started over. "That Iris, for instance," I said haltingly. "She's a fine lady. She, uh, would be the mother, of course."

Jessie chuckled and let me flop around, watching as my face turned red. I dug in and tried again. "That makes you the daughter, of course, and I'm, well, what I'm trying to say is..."

She finally put me out of my misery and leaned in to give me a long kiss. "Are you trying to say that I'm the only one you've got your eye on? Is that what you're trying to say? Because I like the sound of that, Ash McKinnon."

I heaved a sigh of relief. "That's what I'm trying to say. There's nothing in my life I've liked better than this time I've spent at your ranch. And it's not just because I'm an old country boy at heart. It's because of you." I searched for something else to say, then decided to quit while I was ahead. The look in Jessie's eyes told me I'd managed to say what I needed to.

I'd have to say I don't remember a whole lot about the lunch, but I won't forget the couple hours we spent eating the lunch and cuddling on that blanket. It was cold, after all. We had to stay warm, didn't we?

We rode back to the ranch a couple hours later and found Kyle waving a piece of paper at us as we came into the yard. "Telegram from Mr. Stone!" he shouted. "He got the horse thief and found our horses. The horses will come in to Temple on tomorrow's train!"

We swung down, and Kyle handed me the telegram. It was from Captain McDonald, telling me that Stone had caught up with the horse rustler, or one of them, at the train yard in Dennison, and had killed him in a shootout. The man's boot prints matched the ones Red had traced, so the dead man was likely Red's killer. The recovered horses were coming to Temple on tomorrow's train.

I handed the telegram to Jessie, knowing there was grim satisfaction in my eyes at realizing that the man who murdered my old friend Red had met his end by drawing on my old friend and partner Mike Stone.

We gathered around the table in the kitchen, trying to decide who would go into Temple to get the horses. Jessie, Kyle, and I were all volunteering to go, but I had some concerns about going in myself and leaving the family to watch over the ranch. Jessie finally convinced me that they would all be fine, considering that they had caught the horse rustler. I argued that somebody else might be out there waiting to try again, but I had to admit that it had been quiet around here for quite a while. If there were other rustlers still out there, they had probably moved on. Besides, I would be back by tomorrow night.

Jessie saw Ash off in the early morning light. He was mounted on the horse he'd been riding when he first came to the ranch. She smiled as he waved goodbye and headed out the gate. She planned to make the chestnut gelding a present to him when the time came for him to move on to a different assignment. She hoped she would still see that gelding in her corral often. She was pretty sure he would come back to see her when he could.

Jessie walked into the kitchen. Iris saw the smile on her daughter's face and chuckled knowingly as she handed off a cup of coffee. Jessie had given up protesting when Iris teased her about Ash. She knew the mutual interest was perfectly obvious to her family, and there didn't seem to be any point in denying it. The fact that she couldn't stop smiling was a dead giveaway.

The family settled down to breakfast, and Jessie and Kyle discussed what had to be done today. The family garden needed to be hoed and planted with potatoes and onions. That was the least favorite job for both Jessie and Kyle. The fences also needed to be checked today after last night's heavy wind. When both Jessie and Kyle had volunteered for the fence line job, Iris sighed and went over to break a piece of straw off the broom leaning in the corner. She knew from experience there was only one way to settle this.

Iris turned her back and broke the straw into two pieces—one shorter and one longer. She palmed both pieces in her hand and turned around. "OK, you two," she announced. "Choose one."

When Kyle went first and drew the short straw, Jessie threw one hand in the air in celebration, then patted her brother on the back. "Make sure you get all those weeds out first," she reminded him. Seeing the defeated look on his face, she relented slightly. "I'll do the first weeding after you're done with planting," she promised. Then she went outside to saddle up.

As she travelled farther from the house and climbed a little in elevation, moving toward the back of the property, Jessie realized that the wind must have been stronger than she had realized. She had taken the first watch on the back porch, and the wind hadn't really kicked up that much by the time she was sound asleep. Now, she began to see large tree limbs down. She pulled up short when she saw what she had been hoping she wouldn't.

An old, fairly large oak tree had blown down and had landed squarely across the fence on the east side of the pasture. The small herd of about fifty head of cattle had drifted across the fence line and scattered out. Jessie sighed and sized up the situation. She would need Kyle's help to herd the cattle back into the pasture and repair the fence. She reined her horse around and started back for the house.

Ike and Slade had been at the ranch for a day, arguing back and forth over how they were going to steal that stallion. After Ike had explained the difficulties during the first try, Slade was arguing against trying to steal the horse at all. Ike then asked his partner if he, Slade, wanted to explain to Holt why they hadn't stolen the stallion. Slade thought about the two tied-down guns that Holt liked to wear and agreed that they should try to steal it.

The main problem, as they saw it, was the stallion himself. He was a fast, powerful horse, and they were likely to each have to drop a lasso over him to lead him out of there. Watching the house last night, they had learned that there was a guard posted on the back porch all night. Now it was an arithmetic problem. They needed two people to steal the horse and one person to deal with the guard on the porch. Neither one of them liked the odds.

The situation had gotten a little brighter this morning when the Ranger had ridden off at first light. Then, the girl had ridden out shortly later, leaving only the boy, digging in the garden, and the woman, somewhere in the house. Still, it was now broad daylight, and nobody in their right mind, they agreed, tried to rustle horses in broad daylight. Especially, they agreed, when horse thieves generally got hung in Texas.

They were hunkered down in the trees to the west of the corral when the thunder of hooves told them the girl was coming back to the ranch at a gallop. They saw her ride up, waving at the boy and heard the words "fence down". The boy dropped the hoe, dashed into the house for a couple minutes, then came out, saddled up a horse, and rode away with his sister. The mother came out of the house a minute later, propped a shotgun up against the corner of the porch, and began peeling potatoes.

Ike and Slade glanced at each, then began easing back through the trees toward their horses. They wouldn't get a better chance than this.

Chapter Fourteen
Into Thin Air

Iris settled down in a chair on the back porch. She glanced at the shotgun in the corner from time to time—she could use it if she needed to. She picked up a paring knife, glanced out at the corral and started peeling. After about fifteen minutes, she went into the kitchen and started some water boiling on the stove. She went back to the chair on the porch and started in on the potatoes again. About twenty minutes, she estimated, and she could move on to something else. Frequent glances at the corral told her that the horses were undisturbed.

As she leaned over to pick up another potato, Iris heard the unmistakable sound of steps creaking on her left. She froze and glanced over her shoulder. A man was standing there, covering her with a rifle. A bandana covered his face and his hat was pulled down low. Another man appeared on her right. He reached out and picked up the shotgun. He emptied the shells and tossed the empty shotgun over the railing.

"Stay where you are an' take it easy, mum," were the first words either of them spoke. The man on the right advanced toward her. "Put your hands behind your back. Behind the chair. Keep 'em there." She did as she was told. One of them produced a leather strip from his pocket and tied her hands behind the chair. The second one walked over to a sheet drying on the line at the side of the house. He produced a knife and cut two strips from the sheet. He returned to the porch and used one strip as a gag. With the second, he covered her eyes.

Satisfied that the woman would cause them no trouble, Ike and Slade moved to their horses, which they had tethered in the trees. They mounted and moved to the corral. They watched the stallion moving around inside, then both men, remaining mounted, moved into the corral. They both shook out a loop and tossed it at the stallion. Slade missed by a wide margin, but Ike was luckier. His noose settled over the stallion's neck. Two tries later, Slade landed his noose also, and they moved out of the corral. The stallion bucked and plunged behind them, but they kept moving away from the gate. The combined strength of their horses eventually won out, and they began moving steadily as the stallion's bucking slowed. Eventually, they settled down to a steady gallop with the stallion trailing behind them.

They slowed a bit after a while, but kept moving at a brisk pace, trying to put as much distance between themselves and the ranch as they possibly could. Undoubtedly there would be some tracks left behind, but they were counting on the dry ground to make pursuit a little more difficult. It would be a few hours before they came to a stream where they could begin to cover their tracks. Until then, they just wanted to put some miles behind them.

By mid-afternoon they had again slowed the pace, this time to a trot. When they spotted a small stream in front of them, they relaxed. They eased the horses into the stream and splashed through the water for half a mile before emerging on the other side. They felt like things were looking good now, but they wouldn't really feel they were in the clear until they reached the Colorado River.

I returned to the ranch from Temple in the early afternoon and found the place in an uproar. Jessie had saddled two horses— hers and the chestnut gelding. I knew the chestnut gelding was for me, but I wasn't sure where we were going. Kyle was hovering over Iris in the kitchen, asking her if she was OK. Then a glance in the corral told me that the stallion was no longer there, so I now knew why Jessie had saddled our horses. The part I hadn't figured out yet was the concern for Iris. I went in and sat down next to her in the kitchen.

Iris smiled and reached out to take my hand. "Before you ask me, Ash, yes, I'm fine. Two guys showed up on the porch while I was watching the corral and tied me up, then stole the stallion. Mostly I'm upset they got the horse while I was watching." She glanced up at Jessie, who had appeared behind me in the doorway.

"I'm assuming you want to go after these guys," Jessie said, crossing the kitchen to put a hand on my shoulder. "I was mad enough to go after them myself, but common sense told me to wait and even up the odds a little. I have saddled your horse, too." Her face was showing strain, but she bent down to kiss me on the cheek. "And I do mean YOUR horse, by the way."

I looked back at Iris. "You're sure you're fine? I guess the sheriff's assistant will be here before long," I said, remembering the sheriff's offer to send a man out. That conversation seemed like a long time ago now.

Iris waved me away. "I'm fine. They got what they really wanted, so they won't be back. Go get those guys."

I jumped up from the chair so quickly that I almost tipped it over. I righted the chair and waved at Iris as we left the kitchen. Something Jessie had said hit me in a delayed reaction, and I glanced over at her as we trotted toward the horses. "MY horse?" I asked.

Jessie gave me a wan smile and handed me the reins of the chestnut gelding. "This is a fantastic horse," I said, not quite believing he was mine now. We moved toward the corral. "Let's go get your stallion back," I said.

We struck the trail they had left as soon as we pulled away from the corral. It was clear from the tracks left that the stallion was fighting as they led away him; there were chunks of turf torn up where he had kicked and plunged. The trail moved away toward the west, and things seemed to have settled down before too much time had gone by. The three sets of tracks were clear—the stallion was being led by two horses. He was trailing behind them in the center. No doubt both rustlers had a rope around the stallion's neck and had tied the ropes off to their saddle horns.

A little farther along the trail, they seemed to move in a straight line, and judging by the horse's strides, they were proceeding at a full gallop. I knew they couldn't keep that up for too long, but they were making good time, and they knew where they were going. We didn't—we had to follow their trail. I knew we were losing a bit of time for as long as they could proceed at a gallop.

After about an hour, we rested our horses for a while and to give them some water. Jessie looked at me as we re-mounted, then pointed toward the trail in front of us. "Any idea where they are going?" she asked.

I urged the gelding into a canter, not wanting to take my eyes from the tracks. "If I were them," I said, "I'd be heading toward water soon to cover the tracks. Stream, river, something… they have to know this trail is pretty easy to follow."

An hour later, my guess turned out to be true. I would have rather been wrong about this one, but the tracks came to a small stream and disappeared. I knew they had waded the horses along, then left the stream and covered those exit tracks as best they could. There was nothing to do but walk our horses into the stream, watching the banks on both sides for signs of our quarry coming back out of the water.

We eventually found it about a mile downstream. They had dragged some branches over the tracks on the bank and had woven back and forth in the trees near the shore. We sorted that out and struck a small but faint trail left in the woods. I was frustrated because I knew we had probably lost an hour, and we wouldn't have that much more daylight.

Another hour down the trail and they entered another stream, a bigger one this time. We did as we had done before, splashing through the stream, but after following this stream for some time, two things had dawned on me. One, I could hear more water, and I was afraid it was the Colorado River this time. And two, our light was fading rapidly and we would soon need to make camp.

Once again, I was right, and wishing I was wrong. This stream merged with the Colorado River. I knew it would be very difficult to find their exit point from the river, but we would have to try tomorrow. For now, we had to make camp.

We built a small fire, not too far back from the river. I tried to sound more confident than I felt when Jessie asked me about our chances of finding the stallion tomorrow. There was still a decent chance that we could find their tracks leaving the Colorado. A small voice inside me, though, said that things had just gotten a lot tougher.

The night was clear and cold. We laid the bedrolls side by side for warmth, and I told Jessie as we drifted off that we would do better tomorrow. I hoped I was right.

As the sun climbed up higher and higher the next morning, a lot of my confidence was gone. The farther we proceeded down the river, the more both of us were wondering if we'd missed the tracks when they exited. The thought of going back and re-covering the same ground again was unbearable. We called a halt, and I stared out over the expanse of river in front of us, and a sudden thought struck me. I started to talk, then stopped and thought it over a little more. Jessie just watched me and waited.

"Maybe," I said haltingly, "we're going about this the wrong way. Maybe we just need to work on figuring out where the hideout is. We can't be that far away. Maybe the thing to do is start asking the locals around here where rustlers might be hiding out."

Jessie gave a tight smile; her frustration was really showing, and I didn't blame her. "That's great," she said, the doubt sounding heavy in her voice. "But how are we going to do that? Rustlers don't go around telling people where they hide out. And if somebody else that's not a rustler knows, will they really tell us? They won't want these guys coming after them."

A little smile grew on my face. "Maybe we just have to ask the right questions," I said. "We don't ask where rustlers might be hiding out now. Probably only the rustlers know that. What we can do is ask where rustlers and outlaws might have hidden around here in the past. There might be an old-timer or two that knows about that and would be happy to tell us about it. Maybe this place they're using has a history."

A bit of hopefulness appeared in Jesse's eyes. "OK," she said thoughtfully. "Maybe that could work. But where are we going to find old-timers that want to talk to us about horse rustlers and hideouts?"

The smile kept growing until it was a full-blown grin on my face. "That," I told her, "is what saloons are for."

Pendleton found he was deeply disturbed by the presence of Wills' "fixer", Shaw. The man had shown up unannounced at the train station that afternoon and stated that the two of them would have a talk about Lance. There was no shred of a request in what he said—he had simply informed Pendleton it would be happening. Then he had clearly expected Pendleton to walk out on his job for the talk. When Pendleton had insisted it would wait until he was off work, there had been a long and uncomfortable stare-down. Shaw had finally mumbled something about meeting him at the saloon and walked out.

Now Shaw slugged down a shot of whiskey and stared across the table. He reminded Pendleton of a rattlesnake staring at its prey. Shaw waved the shot glass at a waiter, then went back to staring at Pendleton. "I need to know where this guy Lance lives."

"Why?" Pendleton didn't really expect to get an answer to his question, but he was stalling for a little time. He had to decide what would happen if he refused to give the information. He had the uncomfortable feeling he wouldn't live very long if that happened. He also had the feeling he would never see it coming. He would just be dead.

"Boss said to come and get it from you." Shaw got his refill and threw it down instantly. He wiped his sleeve across his mouth and went back to the rattlesnake stare.

Pendleton took a pull from his beer and decided. He wanted to live. Lance could fend for himself. He took another glance at Shaw. Lance would probably never have the chance to fend for himself.

"Round Rock, north of Austin." He fished in his pocket for the address he had written down and brought with him. He slid it across the table and watched as Shaw glanced at it, then shoved it in his pocket. Pendleton tried another question: "What is happening?" He had little hope of getting an answer to that question, and he didn't.

Shaw shrugged and stood up. He didn't bother leaving any money to pay for the whiskey. "Ask The Boss yourself," he said, and then he disappeared through the batwing doors.

Pendleton stayed at the saloon for quite a while after Shaw left. He switched to whiskey, but it didn't help all that much. Something must have gone wrong with this operation, and Wills had clearly got rid of anybody he couldn't trust. The big question, of course, was whether he, Pendleton, was among those people that Wills would decide couldn't be trusted. Pendleton stayed at the saloon and drank until he could barely find his way home. He crashed through the doorway and fell onto his mattress. His brain was working just enough to tell him he would have a big decision to make by morning.

In fact, by the time the morning sunlight coming through his one window finally did its job and woke him up, he wasn't feeling any better than last night. His brain was barely working, that was for sure. He rose, moaning with each step, and fumbled around until he had a cup of coffee strong enough to take the paint off the walls. Well, if he'd had any paint on the walls, the coffee would take it off.

He lurched over to the table and slumped over it with his coffee in front of him. He took a few scalding hot sips and waited for some cobwebs to clear from his brain. He assembled the facts in his head. He had saved a pretty fair amount of money from working this racket with Wills. He certainly hadn't spent it on any luxuries. He had known, in the back of his mind, that Wills was ruthless. Pendleton was pretty ruthless himself, but he didn't have the people to do his dirty work like Wills. Maybe that was a mistake on his part.

He had the same gut feeling that he'd had last night—that Wills was getting rid of people he didn't trust. Pendleton wasn't one of those people yet, but he had a feeling it was only a matter of time. He really didn't think there would be any more stolen horses passing through to help fatten his wallet, and he really didn't care about the railroad job. That left only one conclusion: it was time for him to pull up stakes and get out of here. Out of Wills' reach.

He was a careful man, and he knew how to walk away. He would ride north to Dallas and catch a train ride on the Texas and Pacific Railroad to El Paso. That might be far enough to get away from Wills, or it might not be. He would go on to California if he needed to. The money he'd saved was buried out back. Part of him acknowledged that the bank was a safer place, but the rest of him said that he might need the money in a hurry with nobody at the bank taking notice. You just couldn't trust people not to run their mouths.

Mind made up, he walked outside to the old wreck of a barn he had out back and saddled his horse. It wasn't much of a horse, but he just needed to get to Dallas. He would stay out of sight as much as possible on the way up there. That done, he picked up the shovel in the corner and walked out to the spot where he had buried his money. Being careful was about to pay off. Next time, maybe he needed to get himself a cutthroat like Shaw. It was something to think about.

Chapter Fifteen
Unearthing the Past

Shaw had been following Lance for two days now. Finding him had been pretty easy after getting an address from Pendleton. Round Rock wasn't a big place. Wills had been clear that Lance had to go away. Shaw had no illusions about what that meant, and he never questioned Wills. The money was too good. He had to put up with an occasional tantrum, but that was easy enough. He'd never really had it so good for getting so little work done.

There was really just one big reason why he hadn't done this job yet. The first was, he had to kill Lance and get away without getting shot or having a posse on his trail. The first morning, for instance, Lance had been in town the entire morning. Like most small towns, the businesses were pretty much on one main street. The jail and sheriff's office were pretty close to everything else in town. He could afford to wait for a better chance to do this and still ride away with no bullet holes in him.

That problem had been solved yesterday afternoon. Lance had mounted up and ridden out of town, heading north. Shaw had followed at a distance, just waiting for a good shot. Lance had ridden for quite some time, stopping by the railroad tracks just south of the town of Georgetown. Shaw could see that Lance had stopped at a water stop for the railroad. He seemed to wait for a train. Shaw, sensing his opportunity, had veered off into the woods and found a spot where he could rest his rifle over a low-hanging limb. He was preparing for a shot when he heard the whistle of a train. He watched as Lance ducked behind a rail fence, then he noticed that Lance was keeping an eye on the train as it approached.

The train stopped and began taking on water. Shaw watched in curiosity as the door of the express car opened. He saw Lance getting to his feet, then ducking back down behind the rail fence. Shaw nearly laughed out loud. There was an armed guard on the express car. Lance must have planned to rob the train at the water siding. The armed guard had convinced him that it wasn't such a good idea. Forty- five minutes later, the train rolled away and Lance came out from his hiding spot. He mounted up and rode back toward Round Rock. Shaw let him go.

He still planned to do his job, but holding up the train while it was stopped didn't seem like such a bad idea. For all he knew, Lance was out here every day, trying to pick the right train. Shaw would give it one more day. Maybe an armed guard would do his job for him, or maybe he would just rob Lance after Lance robbed the train, then get rid of him. One more day wouldn't matter that much. If he could make a little money on the side, Wills didn't need to know about it.

As he suspected, the next day played out much like the day before. Lance rode out in the early afternoon and hid out at the water siding. Shaw settled down with his rifle resting across the same branch, hidden back in the trees, and awaited developments. The whistle sounded shortly, and the train rolled around the bend and into view.

This time, things played out differently. The train stopped and took on water. The engineer climbed down and walked alongside the train, apparently just stretching and taking a walk. When he did, Lance came out from his hiding spot and pulled a gun on the engineer. They went to the express car where Lance rapped loudly on the door and demanded that the door be opened.

There was some shouting back and forth for a while. Shaw couldn't really understand the words, but it was obvious that the man inside didn't want to open up. After a while the engineer shouted, and the door rolled open. Lance reversed his gun and struck the engineer on the head with the gun butt. The engineer slumped to the ground and Lance stepped inside the car. After several minutes went by, he came out carrying a burlap bag. He sprinted over to his horse and mounted up.

Mass confusion prevailed. As Lance rode away, a young guy showed up in the express car doorway and took a couple shots at Lance as he rode past. Lance stopped and fired back, but nobody seemed to hit anything. A couple more shots sounded, and Shaw decided this was getting too messy. He couldn't wait and take the money from Lance. He needed to do his job and get out of there.

He sighted down the barrel of his rifle. Lance was half-turned away from him, firing again at the doorway of the car where the kid seemed to duck in and out, taking an occasional shot. Shaw let his breath out slowly, then squeezed off his shot. Lance jerked backwards, then tumbled out of the saddle and lay still on the ground.

Shaw turned, trotted to his horse, and mounted. He hesitated for just a moment, looking back at what was going on at the train siding. The kid had come out of the express car, waving his pistol in the air. A few people spilled out of the train, and they seemed to congratulate the express car kid on shooting the robber. Shaw smiled grimly, then retreated into the trees. If they thought the kid had shot Lance, it was better for him. Nobody would look for him.

The first thing he wanted to do was to get away cleanly. He stayed under the cover of the trees for a while, then finally crossed the tracks and struck the road north. He would stay with the road for a while, then turn west toward the cave. He wasn't exactly sure what Wills wanted him to do there, but he would check things out. If Wills didn't show up or send someone with a message for him, he would go on back to San Antonio after a couple days at Longhorn Cave.

Mike Stone reined in his horse at the edge of the town of Scyene. The sheriff had taken care of things in Dennison after the shooting of Holt and the recovery of the Maitlin horses. A short train ride to Dallas, and overnight stay, and then an hour's ride to the east had brought Stone to Scyene. He surveyed the main street, which was named Scyene Road. He rode along the street until he spotted a café, where he decided to stop off for breakfast.

Taking a table near the window, he pulled out a couple pieces of paper and a pencil, making a few notes about what he knew so far. Scyene had a population now of around 250 people, which was down a little from what it had been at its peak. The town had refused to build a depot for the railroad and seemed to be declining now as a result. They had built the depot in nearby Mesquite.

Stone knew that Myra Maybelle Shirley, or May Shirley, had come to Scyene maybe twenty years earlier, and had lived near the Younger family. She had also known the James family in Missouri, though she didn't seem to have had any part in the James-Younger robberies. Neither family seemed to be around here now, though he thought it would be worth checking around near the farms where they had lived.

A café server interrupted him briefly to bring coffee and to take his order. When she left, he began scratching a few more notes on the paper. May Shirley, now known as Belle Starr, had come here at around age 18, then married a man named Jim Reed two years later. Reed, who had known the Starr family, had been killed in a holdup about six years after marrying May Shirley. Her connection with Sam Starr came a couple years after that. She had married him and moved to the Territory.

Stone decided that the best thing would be to look for friends and acquaintances of May Shirley during those two years after she came to Scyene; before she married Jim Reed. Maybe there was a connection from those early years. If he turned up nothing there, maybe there was someone she and Jim Reed had both known during that timeframe of fifteen to twenty years ago.

Where to start? That was the question. He could try the saloon, but he needed to find someone who had been a friend or acquaintance of May Shirley. The saloon didn't sound like a good place to find somebody like that. He eyed the server as she came back to get his money for the breakfast. Maybe he could start by asking her.

He put a couple of coins on the table, then held out a hand to stop her as she walked away with the money. "Could I ask you a question?" She stopped and waited, saying nothing. Her expression also told him nothing.

"I'm wondering where I could find someone who knew May Shirley, maybe fifteen or twenty years ago." When he got a blank look, he tried again: "Folks call her Belle Starr now, but she was May Shirley or Myra Shirley back then."

The expression turned from blank to slightly suspicious. She glanced at the badge on his chest, then seemed to stop and think about the question. She shrugged. "I didn't know her at all. She's a little older than me. I have an uncle and a neighbor who talk about her from time to time. You could find them both at the lodge tonight." She pointed across the street.

Stone looked across the street and saw a Masonic Lodge. It didn't seem much better than the saloon as a place for asking questions, but he could give it a try. He looked back at the server hopefully. "Can you tell me where she lived when she was here?"

"Sorry." She walked away to take an order from a couple who had just arrived.

After stopping several people on their way down Scyene Road, Stone was finally directed to two small neighboring farms on the east side of Scyene. Here, he was told, was where the Shirley and Younger families had lived during their days in Scyene.

He knocked at the door of the first house for a long time, hearing no answer from inside. Walking around the corner, he found an older woman weeding in the garden. She stopped and watched as he crossed the yard toward her.

She said nothing as he introduced himself and ignored the handshake he offered. She waited impatiently as he explained that he was looking for someone who had known Belle Starr as a young woman. Her expression hardened at the mention of the name.

"You some newspaper fella, tryin' to get a story again? How many times are you people gonna bother me?"

She was building to a full-fledged tirade when Stone stopped her by waving his arms and pointing at his badge. She subsided only slightly, then ignored all further questions as she went back to hoeing her garden. "Don't know nothin'" she informed him over her shoulder.

Stone got only slightly better reception at the next door, and nothing more in the way of answers. By early evening, he was getting thoroughly discouraged. He decided to try the Masonic Lodge. He had no intention of interrupting their meeting, but maybe he could meet somebody on their way in if he waited out in front of the lodge.

Finally, his luck changed. A man coming in for the meeting stopped to answer his questions and directed him to another man who turned out to be the uncle of the woman who had served him in the café. He stroked his beard thoughtfully when Stone asked for anybody who had known Belle Starr.

"Old lady Greer," he said, pointing down the street. "White house with the pink shutters. She was kind to May Shirley, and May didn't have many friends. Ask old lady Greer. Watch out for the fruitcake, though." He chuckled as he walked into the lodge building.

Not sure what that last remark meant, Stone walked down the street to the house they had directed him to. A wizened old lady answered the door and squinted at him as he explained why he had come. Her eyes lighted up at the mention of Belle Starr/May Shirley and she threw the door open, then waved him to a table in the kitchen.

"May Shirley, huh?" The voice was hoarse and sounded a little like a croak. She hovered over him, offering a drink, which Stone declined. "No whiskey?" She sounded very disappointed and poured one for herself.

"OK," she conceded. "No whiskey. You got to have some of my fruit cake, though." She dropped a loaf of something onto the table. Stone pulled back slightly when he heard the solid *thunk* of the loaf hitting the wooden table. She produced a knife and began to saw away at it.

When she had hacked off a piece of the cake, she dropped it onto a plate and pushed the plate in front of Stone. He had to admit that it smelled good and didn't look too bad, but the sound of the single piece thumping down onto the plate had him a little scared. He picked up a fork and prodded at it. Seeing a slightly hurt look on her face, he took a bite, mainly just to keep her talking.

Old lady Greer settled down into a chair opposite Stone and finished off her whiskey. "Belle Starr," she reminisced in a gravelly voice. "She were somethin'. Rode up and down the street in that black velvet ridin' outfit, shootin' off them pistols. She were really somethin'." She reached around for the whiskey bottle again. Stone couldn't help but notice that she wasn't eating the cake. It was feeling a little heavy in his stomach, but he had to keep her talking. He swallowed another piece.

"Didn't have many friends, she sure didn't. She liked to come over here from time to time, an' I'd always talk to her. Didn't have no boy takin' a shine to her, not till that no-good Jim Reed. Can't blame the boys, though. All that shootin' and cussin' and spittin' she always done. And that black velvet..." Old lady Greer shook her head and lapsed into silence.

Stone took a deep breath and swallowed two more bites. "Good cake," he lied. His stomach was complaining.

Old lady Greer brightened up noticeably. "I soak it in rum. That there's the secret," she confided. "Let's see now, May Shirley. She taken up with the no-account Jim Reed, an' then Sam Starr. I don't guess no other boys was interested, though. Them other two used to hang around with her, but I don't think they was up to no good, neither."

Stone's attention homed in on her immediately. "What other two?" he asked. She looked at him blankly, then looked at the cake on his plate. Stone shoveled down another bite.

"Them other two... what was their names?" she mumbled to herself. "One of 'em was Pendleton... Ed Pendleton, I think. The other was Mort Wilson. He wasn't no good, neither. I think maybe the three of them was rustlin' cows or horses or they was up to some kind of no good back then. Pendleton was the smart one. Wilson fancied hisself to be the leader. May should've stayed away from them, too."

Stone put the fork down and leaned forward. She was starting to fade out, probably from that third shot of whiskey. "What became of those two? Do you ever hear anything about Pendleton or Wilson?"

She roused herself briefly and shook her head. "Haven't heard nothin' about Pendleton," she said. She gazed blankly at the opposite wall. "Wilson, I heard he don't exackly go by that name no more. Heard he got hisself elected to somethin'. Mayor, or sheriff, or senator, or somethin'. I still say he ain't no good." Her eyes closed and her head slid down onto the table. Moments later, there was a loud snoring noise.

Stone let himself out and walked over to his horse. He swung aboard and moaned slightly as he did so. Tomorrow, he would send a telegram to McDonald. Meanwhile, he steered his horse toward the saloon. Maybe some whiskey would soak up some of that fruitcake. McDonald would never appreciate what he had gone through to get this information. How much did that cake weigh, anyway? Ten pounds?

Back in Austin, McDonald stopped off at the telegraph office and sorted through three messages. He set aside two of them. The third message, he saw, was from Mike Stone. He opened it and glanced at it briefly. The names Pendleton and Wilson meant nothing to him, but he felt strongly that he needed to follow up on it. He would do that himself, he decided. He dashed off a message to Stone, telling him that he would follow up personally. He paused for a minute, tapping his pencil thoughtfully on the counter. He finished by telling Stone to return to Austin.

Grabbing up his bag, he made a dash for the train station, just down the street. He was catching a train to San Antonio this morning to see if he could get any clues about who had sent that anonymous telegram to tip him off about Holt. Something really didn't smell right about that one. He had to get to the bottom of it.

A train whistle sounded, and he picked up the pace to a full-out sprint. He swung aboard just in time and plopped down onto one bench. With any luck, he would be home tonight, but he wasn't counting on it. He had a strong hunch about this. He would stay in San Antonio as long as he needed to.

Chapter Sixteen
Gentry

We struck a trail south along the banks of the Colorado. I could tell that losing her prize stallion was weighing heavily on Jessie, and I questioned whether my plan was going to work. The trail of the rustlers was only growing colder by the hour, and they had succeeded with as many robberies as they had pulled off because they were good at covering their tracks and moving the horses. We travelled south for a day, pausing only occasionally when we spotted tracks near the river bank. By evening, nothing had panned out, but we came to railroad tracks running east-west. We stopped to talk things over for a while and agreed that in the morning we would follow the railroad tracks east to the nearest town. Maybe there we could pick up a clue about where rustlers might hide out in this area.

We made dinner over a small fire, then we leaned back against a log, covered by a blanket against the evening chill. I wondered what Jessie would do if we couldn't find the stallion, but didn't want to ask. I got up to put a little more wood on the fire, and she seemed to guess at my thoughts.

"I'll always have that ranch," she said thoughtfully. "At least, as long as I'm able to keep things running and hold on to it. It was my Dad's dream, and it's what my family does now. The horse breeding I was doing with that stallion was what I loved doing, but I can still breed and sell mustangs for cowboys, and probably graze a few more head of cattle than I have been. I can keep it going."

I returned and sat next to her in front of the fire again. I thought about my time in Texas, spent on a cattle drive and working with the Rangers. "Well," I said eventually, "you'll always have a place that's home. That's what I miss the most since leaving Tennessee. Home and family."

She reached under the blankets and took my hand. "That's right," she said. "You don't have any family in Texas, do you?"

"No," I said regretfully. "What family I have left is all back in Tennessee."

She gave my hand a squeeze under the blankets. "You never know," she said. "Maybe we can do something about that."

The fire burned down after a while, and the evening grew colder. We laid out bedrolls near the coals and fell asleep, hoping tomorrow would bring us closer to finding that Arabian stallion.

The railroad tracks led us east to a town called Burnet the next morning. I can't say I'd heard of it, but I hadn't been in Texas all that long. It was a pretty small little town, but the local news was that the Austin and Northwestern Railroad had come to town, and things were busy because of the railroad. They had built the tracks from Austin to Burnet, and they were building more tracks to the north, up to the town of Llano. So far as I could tell, there weren't many trains going through yet, but there were jobs for track layers and such. They even had themselves a new telegraph office, and they were building a hotel.

We stopped for breakfast at the only café I could see in town, and I figured that was as good a place as any to ask questions, seeing as how the saloon wouldn't get busy until later. We got disappointed in a hurry though, as the girl that brought our breakfast just shook her head and left when I asked a couple questions. The other two tables had railroad workers who had only come here a couple months before. It was getting hard to shake off the discouragement and the feeling that the rustlers had simply vanished. Again. They were good at it.

We killed some time until the early afternoon, then went down to the saloon. There were only three or four people in there, but the owner had a tip for us. "You need to talk to Gentry," he told us. "Old rascally coot, has a little spread west of here that don't keep him nearly busy enough. That's why he's in here every night. I think he might have rode the outlaw trail hisself, back in the day. He might tell you somethin' or he might not, but you could ask him yourself in a couple hours."

Gentry came in as promised a couple hours later, thumbs hooked behind his suspenders, slumped over slightly as he made his way to a table in the corner. His face was leathery from many hours spent in the sun; the crow's feet at the corners of his eyes were deep and pronounced. He looked up, only mildly curious, as Jessie and I approached.

"Can we ask what you know about outlaws who've been around these parts?" I began. "Maybe horse rustlers who've been around here?"

Gentry glanced away from me as a beer was brought to the table. He glanced at Jessie, then back at me. He drained half the beer in one gulp. "Don't know nothin' about rustlers." He waved for another beer. "Horse thieves get hung."

"Outlaws, then. Have there ever been any outlaws working these parts?" He hesitated, and I tossed a coin onto the table. "I'll buy you a couple," I said.

He shrugged and waved at the table. I held a chair for Jessie and dragged another one over for myself.

"Don't know nothin' about outlaws around here lately," he said. "Maybe there was a few several years back, but that probably don't do you no good now." He shoved my money at the boy that brought his beer and drained the new one.

I dropped another piece of silver on the table. "That's OK," I said. "It doesn't have to be recent. What can you tell me? Has anybody used these parts as a hideout?"

It was a shot in the dark, but he stopped with his beer halfway to his lips. He shot a blurry-eyed look at me over the beer, then at my badge. "I might have heard tell of something," he mumbled. "Didn't do no outlawin' myself, you know."

Now we were getting somewhere. "I don't care what you have done or haven't done." I leaned forward. "Tell me what you know."

Gentry seemed to think things over for a minute. I was wondering if I needed to up his order to some whiskey to loosen his lips, but it turned out that one more beer did the job. He looked back and forth between Jessie and me, then put the empty glass down.

"There's a place right near here that was used by outlaws, a time or two. I mean, I…" He seemed to think better of what he started to say. "I mean, I heard tell, is all," he said evasively. I waved my hand in frustration.

"There's a cave," he said finally. "Rebs used it to make gunpowder durin' the war. Sam Bass used it as a hideout, they say. Rode their horses right in there, to hide out. That's what I heard, anyway. Folks say he hid two million dollars in there one time, but that ain't true. I don't believe it no ways," he amended.

The part about riding horses into the cave had our attention. I glanced at Jessie, trying to keep the excitement out of my voice. "Where is the cave?"

Gentry waved his arm vaguely. "West of here. Ride west. It's out past my spread. Easy to miss, though."

"Will you take us there?" I asked. I was aware of Jessie's hand tightening on my arm.

Gentry immediately shook his head. "Nope." I asked again, and he shook his head again. He moved to get up, and I wondered what else he might know about that cave. I dropped the subject, bought him one more beer, then moved to another table with Jessie.

"He's scared, I think," I told Jessie. "He's afraid of somebody that's been in that cave. Maybe afraid of somebody that's using it now." I drummed the tabletop in frustration. "That place could take a while to find."

Gentry stood up to leave, and Jessie rose and walked across to stop him before he could get to the door. "I run a small ranch with my mother and my brother," she told him. "The most valuable thing by far that I had on that ranch was an Arabian stallion. He was stolen, and it will be hard for us without him. Can't you help us?"

Gentry looked at Jessie for a long moment, then stared at the floor. "OK," he agreed. "You come out to my place in the morning, and I'll help. Bud, over there, can tell you how to get to my place." He pointed at the barkeeper, then left.

McDonald leaned back against the seat and waited for his breathing to come back to normal. It was another sign he was sitting down behind the desk too much—running for the train had left him completely winded. He stared out the window. It wasn't too long ago he would have been riding his horse down here to San Antonio. He preferred to ride his horse, but he had to admit the trains were faster. It made it a little easier for the Rangers to get around, too. The train tracks were being laid everywhere. Unfortunately, it also made it easier for the outlaws to get around.

He pulled a stack of papers out of his bag and started to read. He made a mental note to tell the governor he wanted to go back out and do his work from the back of his horse. There had to be somebody who could stay in Austin and do his job. He'd only worked this job as long as he had at the governor's insistence. A new job, the governor had called it. Somebody else could have it as far as he was concerned.

After a while he put the papers away, except for Stone's telegram from Scyene. He studied it again. The names Pendleton and Wilson still meant nothing, but Stone had passed along a comment from the woman in Scyene that Wilson had gotten himself elected to something. McDonald tapped the message thoughtfully on his knee. He shuffled through his papers again and pulled out a list of statewide elected officials for Texas. He had requested it a few days ago, back in Austin. He looked at the list again. Neither name was on there.

He stuffed the papers back in the bag when the whistle sounded in San Antonio. He hopped down, pulled out the slip of paper with the telegraph office address, and immediately asked directions. It turned out to be a walk of about a mile, but that didn't bother him. He liked to walk.

A bell sounded quietly when he entered the office, and a clerk looked up from behind the desk. McDonald walked across the room, holding the anonymous telegram he had received, tipping him off about Holt. The clerk held out his hand to take the message from him. He prepared to send it, then looked up in confusion. "Uh, what do you want me to do with this, sir?"

McDonald leaned against the counter. "Somebody in your Austin office where I received this message said that it was sent from here. Was it you that sent this message?"

The clerk glanced back down at the telegram and nodded his head. "Yes sir, I sent this message. It has my initials on it." He looked back up, still wearing a look of confusion.

McDonald reached out and took the telegram back. "What I need to know is, can you remember anything about the man who sent this? Anything at all that you can tell me would be helpful."

The clerk reached for the message again, and McDonald gave it to him. "Sent two days ago," the clerk said, mainly to himself. He tapped the paper on the countertop and thought. "I remember only a little. I hadn't ever seen him in here before, I'm certain. He was tall— maybe your height. Slim."

"Age?" McDonald asked.

He stared at the countertop, shaking his head slowly. "Hard to remember, sir. Maybe forty or so." He handed the message back, spreading his hands in an apologetic gesture. "Sorry, there's just nothing else I can remember."

McDonald folded up the telegram, thanked the clerk, and let himself out the door of the office. He dawdled along the street, trying to focus his thoughts. That had been little to move forward with. He walked past the county courthouse and stared at it blankly for a moment. Stone's message said that the man Wilson had gotten himself elected to something. He moved along a little farther, passing the mayor's office, then a small office for city records. He stopped and retraced his steps.

The clerk in the records office looked at him in confusion when he made his request. The man centered his glasses on his nose and repeated McDonald's request. "Elected officials in San Antonio, sir? Elected to what, exactly?"

"Elected to any city offices. You'd have that, wouldn't you?" The clerk nodded slowly. "Yes, most of them, anyway." He eyed McDonald's badge, then nodded again. "I'll make a list of all the elected city officials for San Antonio. Can you check back with me in the morning?"

McDonald thanked the man, then made the same request at the county courthouse for anyone elected to a county office. The clerk there also promised to have a list in the morning.

Feeling somewhat better, McDonald found a place to stay for the night. He would go back to Austin tomorrow.

Milo Wills looked up as Shaw came into his office and slumped down in a chair in the corner. There were a couple things about Shaw, Wills reflected, that really irritated him, and he had just seen two of them. First, Shaw always came in without knocking, and second, he didn't bother to speak to Wills or even look at him. Wills stared at him for several seconds without result, then curiosity got the better of him.

"How's our friend Lance doing?" he rasped, not bothering to look at Shaw. Two could play this game.

"You won't see Lance no more," Shaw said in an indifferent tone. "He got shot during a train robbery." He glanced up, gratified to see the astonished look on Will's face. Shaw nodded. "Yep, he was robbing a train durin' a water stop. The kid in the express car thinks he shot Lance, so I got away clean. It was me got him with my rifle."

Wills leaned forward, elbows on his desk, thinking that one over. He felt considerable relief, he realized. Lance was out of the way and nobody could tie it back to him. Holt hadn't been heard from, and he felt good on that score, too. Maybe he could just rebuild this operation with Pendleton. He'd have to make nice to Belle Starr, though. Lost in thought, he mumbled something to Shaw about taking a walk and left the office.

There were a few loose ends he would still have to tie up. Holt had hired a couple of no-accounts to steal the horses and then look after them at Longhorn Cave. He didn't know exactly what had happened to his scout, who'd been out there looking for horse to steal. He felt sure nobody could tie the scout back to him, but he would have to find somebody else. Maybe, he thought, he should just let things settle down for a few months, then restart the whole rustling operation.

Walking down the street, Wills glanced across the road at the telegraph office where he had gone to send the telegram to the Ranger captain, McDonald. He stared at the man coming out of the office, then forced himself to stop staring and keep walking. The man was wearing a badge, and Wills was pretty sure it was Captain McDonald himself. He had been dressed up for an event when they had met, but it looked like McDonald. Wills walked another hundred yards, then looked back to see McDonald going into another building.

Wills took the long route back to his office, then burst through the door. "Pack up what you need and meet me here in fifteen minutes," he growled. "We're leaving town for a while." He grabbed a gun and some papers from his desk, then went home to pack up.

Next morning, Captain McDonald visited both offices from the day before—the county records office and the city records office. Both had given him a list, and he scanned the names eagerly. Disappointment set in when he failed to see a Mort Wilson on either list. He pulled the state list he had brought from Austin, glanced at it briefly, then folded the three together and put them all in his pocket. He crossed the street, headed for a café he had seen down the block.

As he walked, head down, he nearly collided with a shopkeeper who was sweeping the dirt and leaves away from his shop entrance. McDonald looked up, apologized, and started to move on when a sign on the office next door caught his eye. McDonald stepped back and read slowly:

Milo Wills, esq.
Attorney; Texas State Senator

A surge of excitement swept through him as he pulled the lists from his pocket and shuffled through them to find the names he'd brought on the state list from Austin. He kicked himself mentally for not thinking of this before. Wills and Wilson were pretty close, and a lot of men changed their names to hide their past. He whirled back to look at the shopkeeper, pointing at the sign on the window. "Where..."

The shopkeeper looked at the sign, then back at McDonald. "He's gone. Him and that thug that works for him. Done gone yesterday; had a couple horses packed up. I'd say they'll be gone for a while." He finished sweeping and went back inside.

McDonald stared at the shopkeeper's back, then turned and began trotting back to his room at the boarding house. He would get back to Austin on today's train. Mike Stone should come in today. He would get Stone on the trail. Wills, or Wilson, or whatever his name was, could be the key to everything.

Chapter Seventeen
Closing In

Wills slumped in his seat on the train, resisting the urge to kick Shaw, who was sleeping in his seat with apparently no worries in the world. This was the first time Wills had made the trip to Longhorn Cave since beginning the horse stealing operation nearly two years ago. The train tracks to Burnet had been laid since that time. Maybe, he reflected, that was a reason all by itself to get out of the horse stealing business for a while. The train would bring a lot more people to the area. More people meant more chances someone would find the cave.

Wills didn't know the guys that Holt had used to steal horses and hide them. He knew they operated in and around the cave, and he didn't figure they would be hard to find. He would run them off and keep any horses they might have there. If they objected, well, he didn't plan to make it a fair fight. He would make sure he had the drop on them, and besides, that's why he had Shaw. He really didn't plan to let anybody get away from the cave that might identify him later.

After what seemed like an eternity spent chugging north on the rails, someone came by to inform them that the train would shortly arrive in Burnet. They rolled in, and Wills and Shaw disembarked, then retrieved their horses and mounted up. As they rode through Burnet, Wills glanced over and noticed a beautiful young woman standing outside the telegraph office. He tipped his hat to her, and she nodded. Burnet, Wills thought, was a more interesting town than it had been on his last trip up here. But business came first, he reminded himself. They trotted their horses out of town and turned toward Longhorn Cave.

McDonald arrived at his office to find Stone waiting for him. He trotted into the room, waving at Stone to take a seat. McDonald dropped the list of elected officials for the state of Texas in front of Stone, then hauled his chair around the desk to sit beside him. He ran his finger down the list, then stopped at the name of Milo Wills.

"I think this is your boy Mort Wilson," he informed Stone. "People change their names sometimes to hide what they've done. That woman up in Scyene said he'd gotten himself elected to something, right?"

Stone nodded thoughtfully. "She did. Initials are the same; MW either way. Could be him. Where is this guy Milo Wills located?"

McDonald explained how the state senator was located in San Antonio, but had left town in a hurry yesterday. He thumped the desk in frustration at the fact he didn't know where to look now.

Pulling his watch from a pocket, McDonald jumped up and headed for the door.

"I've got to talk to the governor," he said. "You can go on home for a couple hours, if you want to. I'll check for messages after my meeting. If we haven't heard from McKinnon by the time my meeting is over, you can go back to the Maitlin Ranch and see what has been happening there."

Stone followed him out the door, wondering if he had enough time to go home and come back. He decided it was worth it to make the trip.

I took my time in the telegraph office, trying to figure out exactly what I wanted to tell McDonald about where we had gone and why. I settled for saying that the stallion had been stolen from the Maitlin Ranch, and I had followed the trail to the Colorado River, where the trail had gone cold. I tapped the pencil on the countertop for a while, then settled for saying that I believed they could hide the stallion at a place called Longhorn Cave. I could explain the rest of it another time. I started to hand it over to be transmitted, then pulled it back. I added a sentence to say that Longhorn Cave is near the town of Burnet, and there was a guy named Gentry who would guide us. I scanned what I had written one more time, then handed it over to the clerk.

Jessie was waiting on a bench outside the telegraph office when I came out. She linked her arm through mine as we stepped off the boardwalk. We unhitched the horses, but she paused before mounting.

"Do you think we should get some food and supplies before we go out there?" she asked. "You said it could take a while to find it. Maybe we should make sure we can stay for a while and keep looking if we need to."

I agreed, and we made a stop at the general store before leaving town. Jessie picked up some food while I laid in some extra ammunition for both my Colt and Winchester. I figured if these guys had gone to this much trouble to steal the stallion, they probably wouldn't want to give him up peaceably. More time had passed than I had figured on, so we hurried to get back to the horses and on the trail.

We followed the directions they had given me to Gentry's place; we found him about forty-five minutes later, standing on a falling-down porch with his thumbs hooked into his suspenders. He watched us ride up, but there was no smile on his face.

Jessie leaned in to me as we reined in the horses. "Do you think he's had second thoughts about helping us?"

"Looks like it," I mumbled. I kept my eyes locked on his as he came down slowly from the porch.

Like he was reading our thoughts, Gentry looked first at me, then at Jessie. He dropped his eyes to the ground after looking at her, then stared off down the trail behind us. Finally, he cleared his throat, looking back at Jessie.

"I said I'd hep ya, and I will, a little," he said in a soft voice. "I mean, I'll get you close to that cave and point the way for the last bit. That's the best I'll do," he said defiantly. "Take it or leave it."

I exchanged glances with Jessie—we really didn't need to talk about it. I looked off toward the west, assuming that the cave lay in that direction.

"Take us to it," I said.

Gentry mounted up, and we followed him, moving to the west as I had thought we would. None of us said anything; the creak of saddle leather was the only sound to be heard. The ground stayed level for a while, then rose slightly. Stands of oak trees became more frequent and a little thicker. In another fifteen minutes we were weaving in and out among some large boulders, and the terrain became more rugged.

Finally, Gentry stopped and half-turned his horse to face us. He pointed off toward the northwest, then waved his hand in that direction.

"I ain't goin' no further," he announced. "T'ain't gonna be that hard to find it from here. Just keep yore eyes open." He turned and rode off.

I watched his retreating back for a moment, then turned back to look in the direction he had pointed. I started to tell Jessie we could just spread out a few yards apart, and work to the north and west. I stopped halfway through what I was saying and we both ducked down over our saddles when we heard nearby gunshots.

Mike Stone was back in McDonald's office when the door popped open and McDonald walked in, pushing a telegram into Stone's hand.

"Telegram from McKinnon," he said. "Just got it this morning. I think maybe you need to go to this cave."

Puzzled about the cave remark, Stone took the telegram and read it. He hadn't heard of Longhorn Cave, but that's what would make it a good hideout—if very few people knew about it.

"I can take the train to Burnet," Stone said, rising from the chair and grabbing his hat. "What about this Milo Wills guy? Or Mort Wilson, or whatever his name is. Want me to do anything about that?"

McDonald shook his head and dropped into this chair.

"You just go find this cave and see if McKinnon needs any help. If we have a lot of luck, that's where Wills went yesterday. I'll see what I can find out about Senator Wills and where he came from. And Stone... the shopkeeper yesterday said Wills has a thug that works for him. Keep your eyes open and tell McKinnon that goes for him too."

The trip to the train station was a quick ride, then Stone could catch a late morning train to Burnet. McKinnon's telegram had said they were being guided to the cave by a man named Gentry. He would take time to ask around town about Gentry and where he lived. He slid down in the seat and pulled his hat down over his eyes. Today was shaping up to be a long day.

Wills and Shaw were approaching the entrance to Longhorn Cave—Wills felt sure of it. He had last been there a year or two earlier, so he was a little fuzzy on the landmarks, but he knew they were getting close. He pulled Shaw aside and explained his plan for dealing with the two men Holt had used to steal and watch the horses.

"I plan to ride up to the entrance of the cave by myself," he told Shaw. "Your job is to move along beside me, using the boulders for cover. When I run into these two guys, I need you to cover me from someplace where they can't see you." He added an afterthought as Shaw pulled his rifle out of the scabbard. "They don't really need to be around to point us out to the sheriff or Texas Rangers later on."

Shaw dismounted without answering and tethered his horse in a stand of oak trees. He knew what to do. He returned, carrying his rifle, and began moving from boulder to boulder, staying about thirty yards to the left of Wills.

Wills moved forward, holding his horse to a walk to allow Shaw to keep up. He followed a slightly weaving path, staying alert for the cave entrance. He really didn't want to stumble into it. As it was, he nearly stumbled into Holt's men before he found the cave.

Emerging from a stand of trees, eyes scanning from left to right, Wills jerked his horse to a halt suddenly when he saw two men standing in front of him, side-by-side. Wills' horse crow-hopped a time or two at the sudden yank on the reins and Wills soothed the horse as he eyed the two men. Both held rifles in front of them. They pointed the muzzles at the ground, but Wills knew he couldn't make any sudden moves. It wouldn't take that long to bring those rifles to bear.

"Howdy," he said conversationally, resisting the urge to look over his shoulder to see if Shaw was in place. "I'm looking for a lost horse. Wandered out this direction this morning. Either of you boys see a horse wandering around here?"

"Nope." The speaker was the one on the left. He leaned over to spit on the ground. "Long ways for a horse to wander off, mister. You sure he was lost?" He sneered a bit as he asked, and Wills had no doubt these were Holt's horse thieves.

Wills sized up the situation. The one on the left was itching for a fight. He had raised the muzzle of the gun slightly and was trying to stare Wills down. The one on the right still looked to be fairly relaxed. His gun muzzle remained pointed at the ground, but he was scanning the trees and boulders on both sides. That was the smart one, Wills decided. He was more dangerous.

Wills gave the one on the left a disarming smile. "Yep, he just wandered off," he said. "You trying to say I'm a horse thief, mister? Because you sure look like a horse thief to me." He finished with a hard edge to his tone.

It took a second for the words to register. The one on the left had a smirk on his face that changed to anger as the words sunk in. The muzzle of the gun came up, then the man was driven backwards by Shaw's shot. The rifle clattered to the ground, and he slumped sideways, dead instantly from a shot through his chest.

Wills palmed his pistol, prepared for a shot at the second man. Shaw's gun sounded again, but the second man had leaped to the side and dropped behind a boulder. He snapped off a quick shot at Wills, who dove from his horse and crawled behind another boulder. After several seconds passed with no further shots, he eased his head around the base of the boulder for a look. He could hear a faint rustling of leaves and twigs somewhere ahead of him, but the second man seemed to be gone. Wills rose to his feet, remaining crouched behind the boulder, and waved for Shaw to come forward.

Shaw came forward, but Wills chafed at how long it was taking. Eventually Shaw came into view, using the trees and boulders for cover. Wills waved his pistol impatiently, but Shaw ignored him completely, focusing on the ground in front of him until he had worked to a position parallel to the one held by Wills. He continued forward, and Wills moved forward after a moment, lagging a little behind Shaw. He intended to let Shaw take the risks.

Shaw reached the place where the two men had been standing, and Wills covered him from behind a tree while Shaw checked the dead man, then the tracks left by the second man. The two of them followed the tracks for just fifty yards or so, but the prospect of somebody returning the favor and shooting them from cover proved to be too much. They returned to the mouth of the cave. Wills walked inside briefly, then came back out. There were fresh horse droppings inside, but he wasn't going to chase after a horse at this point. The second man, the one who had gotten away—that was more important.

Wills came back to stand beside Shaw, relieved at not getting shot, but not all that happy about that horse thief that got away. He had pretty well decided to order Shaw to go after the man while he himself waited in the cave. He started to say so, irritated that Shaw didn't seem to listen to him.

"Somebody else comin'," Shaw said as he ducked and scrambled to the top of a small rise, taking cover behind a boulder. Wills could see his rifle resting in a niche at the top of the boulder. Wills broke in the other direction, taking cover behind a large oak tree. In a few minutes he could see the man Shaw had seen just a few minutes earlier. He was on foot, leading his horse and coming along slowly. The sunlight reflected off the badge on his chest.

Shaw stayed motionless where he was. The man he'd spotted earlier was still coming forward, although slowly. He turned slightly, giving Shaw a better look at him, and Shaw caught the glint of sunlight reflecting off the badge. He smiled slowly and crouched a bit, shifting just a little to sight down the barrel. Shooting a Ranger would be a first. He was going to enjoy this.

We had drifted in the direction of the gunfire. The more ground we covered, the more worried I became. Not for me. I'd been shot at before and no doubt I would be again, but I was worried for Jesse. Her mother and brother needed her back at the ranch. There was nobody at home waiting for me. I stopped and started to explain why I wanted her to stay back.

"It's dangerous," I began. "We don't know how many of them are out there or who they're shooting at." I could see by the set of her jaw I wasn't getting anywhere.

"I'm coming with you," she said firmly. "Anyway, who's saying they're not coming in this direction and they'll find me here after you're gone?"

Well, she kinda had me there. We really didn't know where these guys were, or what their problem was. Finally, I worked out a compromise with her.

"OK," I said finally. "Come with me, but will you let me go first? Stay off to my side and maybe thirty or forty yards behind me. If anybody draws a shot, I want it to be me. Will you agree to that?"

She thought it over and agreed. We proceeded on horseback for maybe a mile, then we dismounted. I used the trees for cover a little more, and urged Jessie to do the same. She stayed back as I agreed, and I slowly worked my way forward, thinking maybe we were getting close to that cave.

Jessie stayed back as asked, but kept her rifle ready as she moved from tree to tree. There were boulders now as well, and she wove back and forth among them. Things had been quiet for more than a half hour now since they had heard the gunshots, and she wondered if the horse thieves had cleared out and taken the stallion with them.

Moving toward a large boulder, she scanned from left to right, seeing Ash on her left. She swept the ground on her right visually, then froze. She drew a deep breath and moved forward to the boulder in front of her. There was a man ahead of her, maybe sixty yards away, using a boulder for cover as he took aim at Ash. She didn't have much time. She dropped to the ground, laid her rifle across the boulder, and squeezed off a shot.

Chapter Eighteen
Hunters and Hunted

Ike couldn't believe he was still alive. He had spent several months with Slade, stealing horses and hiding them at this cave. He knew he wasn't any smarter than Slade, and he was sure he wasn't any faster with a gun. He liked to think he had a better sense of self-preservation. When the man on the horse had showed up outside the cave, he really wasn't too worried because he and Slade had the numbers in their favor. Slade had a quicker temper, and Ike could tell he was getting ready to shoot the guy. That was OK with him, it saved him from doing the dirty work. When somebody they couldn't see had opened up with a rifle on Slade, Ike had lit out of there like a scared jackrabbit. But, he reminded himself; he was still alive and Slade wasn't.

He hadn't tried to cover his tracks at all. He'd just run in a zig-zag pattern, using trees or rocks for cover if he could. He was surprised they hadn't come after him—he knew he'd made a lot of noise, and it couldn't have been that hard to follow his tracks. Now, he was just lying in some underbrush, peering out through the leaves, not quite believing his own luck.

He was jolted into action when he heard more gunfire coming from the direction of the cave. He wormed out from the underbrush and began running toward his horse. Once in a while he leaped from boulder to boulder in an effort to cover his tracks, but it was a halfhearted effort at best. Mainly he needed to get out of there. Maybe they could occupy themselves with shooting at each other.

In another few minutes he could see his horse. He slowed down, looking in both directions, afraid that somebody lay in ambush, waiting for him to reach his horse. After a brief pause, he knew he had to keep moving. He ran for his horse at full speed, once again hugely relieved when there were no further gunshots. His saddle was back in the cave; no time to mess with that. He untied the rope he had used to tether the horse and leaped up bareback. He trotted away, passing Slade's horse and the Arabian stallion.

He stopped and looked at the stallion. That was one fine horse. Did he dare take it with him? Greed won out, and he untied the Arabian's rope from the tree. The other end was still looped around the stallion's neck, and the horse followed along quietly enough. Ike swung a wide circle around the cave, then settled into a steady trot, headed for Burnet and the railroad.

Thirty minutes later, he was relaxing and congratulate himself. He had pulled off the trail from time to time, checking his back-trail. Nobody seemed to follow him. Maybe those guys were busy, what with another gun battle breaking out before he'd left. He could get a good price for this stallion somewhere and start again.

After another few minutes, as he was drawing close to Burnet, he saw another rider coming down the trail. He pulled his hat low, feeling fairly confident that the other rider couldn't be anybody who would recognize him. He and Slade had kept to themselves around here. He kept his gaze down on the trail, but he sensed that the other rider was slowing down. He risked a glance upward.

Ike's heart sank when he saw that the other man wore a badge. To make matters worse, he really seemed to be looking pretty hard at the stallion. His gaze travelled from the stallion to Ike. Several thoughts raced through Ike's mind at once, but one thought trumped all the others: horse thieves got hung in Texas, and he didn't want to get hung.

Mike Stone had directions to Gentry's house scratched onto a piece of paper, and he pushed his horse along at a brisk pace, following the directions they had given him. He didn't know exactly what Ash had found in Longhorn Cave, and he didn't know if the girl

Jessie was with him, but something told him he needed to get there as soon as he could.

He saw the other rider coming down the trail and thought nothing of it at first. This didn't look to be a well-used trail, but occasional travelers were to be expected, and nothing seemed unusual at first glance. As they drew closer, he noticed that the other man had no saddle, and was leading another horse with a rope he was holding with his left hand. Another look at the horse the man was leading told him this was an exceptional horse. In another instant, Stone knew this could well be the Arabian stallion missing from the Maitlin Ranch.

The other man seemed to mostly stare down at the trail. He pulled his horse slightly to the left, intent on passing Stone without looking at him. Stone moved his horse over to block the path.

"Hold on," said Stone, dismounting slowly, keeping his right hand near his gun belt. He noticed that the other man seemed to be keenly aware of Stone's gun hand.

"I need to have a look at that horse you're leading," Stone said shortly. "Go ahead and dismount."

The other man sat still for a moment, and Stone had the feeling there were several ideas going through his head at once. For an instant, Stone thought he was going to kick his horse in the ribs and make a run for it. Then he seemed to settle down. He shrugged and dismounted. An alarm went off in Stone's head when he saw the man was dismounting on the far side of his horse.

A small voice sounded in Stone's brain: *He's going to shoot under the horse!*

When the other man's feet hit the ground on the far side of his horse, Stone knelt and drew in one motion. When the man's knees bent, Stone knew he'd been right. A gun appeared underneath the horse, and Stone fired. His shot hit the man in the thigh and he pitched backward, his gun going off in the air. The man's horse reared and raced away. Stone could see him now, raising up on one elbow and trying to bring the gun to bear. Stone fired again, and he slumped to the ground.

Stone rose slowly and moved over to the other man, keeping his gun out in front of him. A quick check told him the man was dead. Stone holstered his Colt and looked around. The horses hadn't gone far. His priority, as far as Stone was concerned, was to find McKinnon. He rounded up both horses and tossed the dead man over his horse. Then he led both horses over to a stand of trees and tethered them. He would come back to get them after he knew McKinnon was safe.

I was slipping through the trees and going from boulder to boulder, intent on the path in front of me. I felt pretty sure I could see the cave opening now—just a dark space from where I stood, but there seemed to be some footprints in front of that space. I moved from behind an oak tree, intent on getting a better look, when two rifle shots sounded.

The first shot was fired very close to me. I knew immediately it was Jessie. I registered movement in front. A man tumbled from behind a rock formation, his rifle sliding down through the boulders. The second shot came at the same time, and I felt the impact on my left shoulder. It spun me around and down. A third shot whistled through the air above me. I had the presence of mind to grab my rifle and roll behind a boulder, but it cost me. The pain in my shoulder was so intense I nearly passed out. I curled up behind the rock and fought to stay conscious.

There were a few searching shots as I laid there. A couple of them struck the boulder in front of me, then there was a shot on either side. I knew that he knew where I was, but I also knew the rock protected me in front. Otherwise I would have been dead by now.

I looked around me to size up my situation. There were two boulders protecting me in front, lying side by side, one slightly higher than the other one. I took a breath and crawled slightly to my left, feeling waves of nausea wash over me. There was a slight crevice between the rocks. I swallowed hard and risked a peek between the boulders, fearing the shot from above that might send rock fragments into my eyes.

After a couple quick glances, I realized that he probably couldn't see me watching from between the boulders. He was too far away and above me. I settled down to look for the shooter through that crevice. I felt thirsty, besides the weakness and shock passing over me after the gunshot. I looked longingly at my horse, cropping grass about fifty feet away. I could see my canteen hanging from the saddle horn, but I didn't dare try to call the horse over. My attacker would kill the horse in an instant. I was probably lucky he hadn't thought of it yet.

I settled down and concentrated on looking through that crevice between the rocks, trying to figure out exactly where the shooter was located. For a few minutes, nothing seemed to move. I felt sweat trickling down on my forehead and cheeks, and I knew it wasn't from hot weather. It was a pretty cold winter day, actually. I might not have that much time before I would pass out. That could be the end of both Jessie and me.

In the end, it was the reflection of sunlight off the gun barrel that gave him away. He was in a nest of boulders up there, closed in on three sides, shielding him from both Jessie's position and mine. He was back in the rock's shadow on my right, too far above me to offer a decent shot from where I was laying. I could see only the top of his head, but an idea came to me. I waited for my chance, hoping I would be strong enough when the moment came.

Finally, he seemed to lean away and down. The top of his head disappeared for a moment, and I got to my knees and laid my Winchester across the boulder. When the top of that head came back into view, I laid down several shots in a row into that nest of boulders. I knew how much damage flying rock chips could do. A moment later I heard cursing, and he burst out of the nest of boulders, then he ducked around behind them. I got off one shot that might have grazed him, because I heard a fresh round of cursing, then silence. Now came the hard part.

I had to move and get to a new position. He knew exactly where I was, and he had me completely pinned down here. I needed the ability to raise up and get a clean shot at him without, as Doc Linden would say, getting my fool head shot off. I had spotted a place in front of me with protection from a couple large trees and a long, flat rock, maybe two feet high. The shooter disappeared behind the boulder nest and I got up and broke into a stumbling trot toward my goal. I half tripped, half dove behind the rock. A moan broke from my lips and I passed out for a few seconds.

I came to and rolled closer to the rock. I found myself looking in a different direction, to the right of the nest of boulders I'd been watching before. My eyes widened when I saw Jessie, crouched in a small trough, sheltered by a few rocks and some underbrush. She stayed low, waving her arms to get my attention. When I locked in on her, she pointed toward the shooter's new position.

I scanned the area where she was pointing, and I could see him behind yet another rock. It sheltered him from Jessie and from where I had been lying before, but I could see his shoulder from my new spot. He was facing away from me, and it looked like he was going to try to circle around and come in from the side or from behind us. My eyes travelled along the path he needed to take. There was enough cover that he might just make it. I motioned to Jessie to stay where she was. I would have a clear shot when he moved. I just hoped I would be conscious and able to take it.

Wills crouched in his new spot, knowing he probably couldn't stay there for too long. There were two of them out there, and they both knew how to shoot. He could see Shaw from where he was crouching now, and it wasn't pretty. He had probably raised up just enough for somebody down there to get off a shot at his head, and that's where he'd been hit. Wills shuddered and looked away.

He knew he had hit the one on his right down below. He'd seen the man go down and there was blood on the ground next to where he had taken cover. The man could still shoot, though—blood was dripping from Wills' right cheek where he'd been stung by rock fragments, and there was a long nasty bullet furrow across his back.

The one on the left had been quiet for a while, and Wills was wondering if one of his shots down there had hit the mark. He couldn't stay here for much longer. This had to be finished, one way or the other. The one he'd shot earlier had a badge on his chest, and Wills was assuming he was a Texas Ranger. If there were any more of them around here, he had to get out.

He would make a dash to circle around the one on his left. If he could get down there, off to the side or behind them, he would have the advantage. A sudden rush might just catch them by surprise. He gathered a deep breath and lunged out from behind the rocks.

I worked my way up to my knees and to the left, mainly using one tree for cover. I was partially exposed, but I could see him from this spot, and he was looking the other way. I held the rifle barrel up against the tree to steady it down. My shoulder was throbbing with pain and I knew I had lost a lot of blood. The trickle of sweat had turned into something more like a river, running down my forehead and into my eyes. I ran my sleeve across my face and struggled through waves of dizziness. I had to wait for him to make his move.

There! He came to his feet and broke out from behind the rocks, running in a zig-zag pattern toward the trees on his left. I moved the Winchester slightly and drew a bead on him, following his motion. I drew a breath and exhaled slowly, squeezing the trigger. The shot knocked him down, but he came up on his hands and knees and continued crawling toward the trees. I'd been too weak to hold my shooting position and landed on my back after the shot. The rifle clattered to the ground.

I scrambled to my knees and picked up the Winchester. There was no time to steady it against the tree again. He'd gotten to his feet now and was staggering toward the trees. I brought the Winchester up, sighted in, and squeezed the trigger one more time. He grabbed his chest, fell on his side, then slowly rolled over on his back, staring at the sky.

I slumped to my knees and fell back against the rock I had been using for cover. The surrounding trees seemed to swim in and out of focus. I heard footsteps running toward me, and then I heard Jessie calling my name...

I think I had only been out for a few minutes. Jessie was patting my hand and splashing water on my face. I shook my head to clear my vision and tried to move, but my shoulder was telling me not to try that again. I looked up to see Jessie's beautiful face. My head seemed to be cradled in her lap.

"Stay with me, Ash." She splashed a little more water on my face and smiled when she saw me open my eyes and focus on her. "Stay with me," she repeated.

A smile spread slowly across my face. "When you said to stay with you, did you mean just for now, or did you mean it permanent?"

I closed my eyes and heard a soft chuckle, then felt the cool pressure of her lips against mine. "We can make that happen," she said.

Chapter Nineteen
Home at the Ranch

We were sitting on the back porch in a little swing I had put together with my one good arm. Of course, I had made it to be a swing for two. We could fit in it with a little room to spare, but it seemed like the extra room was never between us when we sat there. Doc Linden had visited this morning and said that my shoulder would heal up just fine. The bullet hadn't hit the bone. He told me to wait a few weeks before I tried to use that arm very much. I pointed out that I'd been hit in the shoulder this time, not the head, and he allowed that I was making some progress in that respect.

We had managed to get me in the saddle that day back at the cave, and we had run into Mike Stone on the trail back to Burnet. We stopped to get the Arabian stallion on the way into town, along with the other member of the horse rustling gang. He'd been in no condition to go anywhere. Five of them were dead, and we knew that Pendleton had left his railroad job in Temple and had disappeared. So far, we had found no sign of him anywhere.

We watched as the stallion and a few mares galloped across the pasture in back of the house. They were no longer confined to the corral, of course, but it seems that Iris had been giving them some carrots most days they had been there, so they were hanging out closer to the house than they had been before all the horse stealing had started. Watching them run was becoming one of my favorite pastimes while I was healing up. One of my favorites, but not my top favorite, of course. That swing for two was awfully nice.

Jessie and I had continued to talk about a future together, and I knew the next step was up to me. The doc had told me I should be able to saddle up and ride after another week, and my first trip was going to be to go into town and find a ring. I had taken Iris into my confidence, and she had told me what size I should get and what kind of rings Jessie liked. Jessie knew something was up and asked me some leading questions once in a while. But a guy has to have a few secrets, doesn't he?

We heard horses coming, and after a few more seconds, Mike Stone and Captain McDonald rode in and tethered their horses at the corral. We had known they were coming. Captain McDonald had sent me a telegraph saying they wanted to talk to me, but he hadn't told me what it was about.

We had set up chairs for them on the porch, and Iris bustled about, getting them coffee and cookies. We made small talk for a few minutes. McDonald told me that Milo Wills and Mort Wilson had in fact turned out to be the same person. It seems that he, Pendleton and Belle Starr had done a little rustling in their days back in Scyene. Belle Starr was, of course, out of our reach up in the Territory. Pendleton had been seen buying a ticket for El Paso, but we didn't know if he was still in the state or not. At any rate, the gang had pretty much been put out of business.

McDonald paused and eyed Jessie and me sitting in the swing, then allowed himself a small smile. "I would ask how you're doing, McKinnon, but you seem to be doing fine."

I glanced over at Jessie, who gave me a smile. "Sometimes, cap'n," I said, "a man just has to make do the best he can." Stone snorted loudly.

McDonald shook his head and chuckled. "Well, anyway," he continued. "We came to talk to you about a couple of changes that we're going to make." He glanced over at Stone, who was watching the horses in the pasture. McDonald looked back at me. "I've been in charge of special projects, reporting to the governor directly, for the last year or so."

I nodded—this wasn't news. I began to wonder what this had to do with me.

"So," McDonald continued, "I guess you know I haven't really wanted to spend so much time behind a desk. I've really been wanting to get back out and command some men in the field, like I used to." He cleared his throat and glanced over at Stone again. "I asked the governor if I could return to doing what I had done before.

He agreed on the condition that I find somebody to replace me." He looked over at Stone again, and it dawned on me.

"You going to have Mike take your place," I said. McDonald nodded. "Captain Stone is now the special assistant to the governor."

My mouth formed the words "Captain Stone," but no sounds came out. I looked back and forth between them. "Congratulations, Mike," I said. "Does this have anything to do with me? It seems like a long way to ride..."

Mike spoke for the first time. "The captain here," he said, pointing at McDonald, "has been pretty much buried trying to keep up with things. He can request help from the other units, but there's been no one else working on this...this special force. I've been told I can have one man to help me. I came to ask you if you'll work with me."

I looked at Jessie, then at Stone, chasing the thoughts around in my head. "It sounds great," I said, "but I've been planning to spend a lot of my time around here. And, well... this is a long way from Austin."

The two of them exchanged glances. They seemed to have thought about it already.

"That's not going to be a problem," Stone said. "We're using the trains more and more to do the job, and you're pretty handy to the railroad lines right where you are. When you need to come into Austin you can, but it might not be all that often."

I took a minute, thinking things over. I looked at Jessie, who nodded and squeezed my hand.

"Come on, Tennessee boy," Stone said, needling me. "What do you say?"

"Well, cap'n, it sounds purty good," I drawled. "Cain't see no problems with it a 'tall."

Stone rolled his eyes. "He's mending just fine," he told Jessie. "He only does that thick Southern country boy accent when he wants to irritate me."

After we'd all had lunch and McDonald and Stone were on their way back to Austin, I walked out to the back porch again, watching that stallion run. Jessie came out and took my hand, standing beside me.

"I really liked that part about wanting to spend your time around here," she whispered. "Are you really going to do that?"

"Let me say it this time," I told her. "We can make that happen."

The End

Made in the USA
Las Vegas, NV
05 March 2021